# BADGE 411

# BADGE 411

*Based on the Actual Experiences of a Probation Officer*

# KURT NIEMANN

ReadersMagnet, LLC

*Badge 411: Based on the Actual Experiences of a Probation Officer*
Copyright © 2022 by Kurt Niemann

Published in the United States of America
ISBN Paperback: 978-1-956780-23-9
ISBN eBook: 978-1-956780-19-2

All rights reserved. No part of this publication may be reproduced, stored in a retrieval system or transmitted in any way by any means, electronic, mechanical, photocopy, recording or otherwise without the prior permission of the author except as provided by USA copyright law.

The opinions expressed by the author are not necessarily those of ReadersMagnet, LLC.

ReadersMagnet, LLC
10620 Treena Street, Suite 230 | San Diego, California, 92131 USA
1.619.354.2643 | www.readersmagnet.com

Book design copyright © 2022 by ReadersMagnet, LLC. All rights reserved.
*Cover design by Ericka Obando*
*Interior design by Mary Mae Romero*

## *About The Author*

The Author is a retired Probation Officer. He served his home State in that capacity for 32 years. His academic background includes a Bachelor of Arts Degree in Sociology and a Master of Science Degree in Criminal Justice. He served in the United States Marine Corps during the years 1955 through 1962. He holds Mixed Martial Arts Black Belts and is a Seventh Level Master.

During a prior marriage, the author was blessed with two wonderful sons. Now, thanks to his current marriage, he has three beautiful stepdaughters as well.

The Author's other main interests include aviation (he is a Certified Commercial Pilot), Black Powder shooting, and visiting antique stores.

# Contents

About The Author .......................... v

Why Did I Write This Book? .................. xv

What Does A Probation Officer Do? ............ xxi

Chapter 1  The Rookie Years................... 1

              Introduction: ...................... 1

              How I Became A Probation Officer..... 2

              The Powder Blue Negligee............ 5

              The Rubber Stamp................. 10

              Baby Ducks ...................... 14

              Happy New Year .................. 14

              The Sick In ....................... 19

              Let's Go Out For Lunch ............ 21

              Gimme My Girlfriend! ............. 23

|  |  |  |
|---|---|---|
|  | Larry | 25 |
|  | Houdini | 28 |
|  | Painter | 29 |
|  | F.y.v.m. | 31 |
|  | "Curly" | 33 |
|  | Curly I: Rookie Cop | 34 |
|  | "Curly" Ii – How We Learn | 37 |
| Chapter 2 | Projects And Barrios | 39 |
|  | Introduction: | 39 |
|  | The Wall | 40 |
|  | BAT LADY | 44 |
|  | On City Retirement | 46 |
|  | Drugs Of Choice | 48 |
|  | Cat Daddy And Batman | 55 |
|  | Strollin' | 57 |
|  | Hit Girl | 60 |
|  | Everybody Has A Story | 63 |

|  |  |
|---|---|
| | The Innocents . . . . . . . . . . . . . . . . . . . 65 |
| | Los Mojados . . . . . . . . . . . . . . . . . . . . 67 |
| | Ms. Pac-Man. . . . . . . . . . . . . . . . . . . . 70 |
| | Cuffing The Cop. . . . . . . . . . . . . . . . . 75 |
| | Shallah. . . . . . . . . . . . . . . . . . . . . . . . . 76 |
| | That Didn't Hurt! . . . . . . . . . . . . . . . . 81 |
| | Tattooed But Not Screwed. . . . . . . . . . 82 |
| | Curly Iii. . . . . . . . . . . . . . . . . . . . . . . . 85 |
| | Curly Iv . . . . . . . . . . . . . . . . . . . . . . . 86 |
| | Curly V . . . . . . . . . . . . . . . . . . . . . . . 87 |
| Chapter 3 | "Inkys:" Those Status Offenders". . . . . . 89 |
| | Introduction: . . . . . . . . . . . . . . . . . . . 89 |
| | What Is An "Inky?". . . . . . . . . . . . . . . 90 |
| | The Drama Triangle . . . . . . . . . . . . . . 92 |
| | Take My Kid---Please! . . . . . . . . . . . . 96 |
| | They Stick Around . . . . . . . . . . . . . . . 98 |
| | The Professional Parents . . . . . . . . . . . 102 |

|  |  |  |
|---|---|---|
|  | Alcoholics | 104 |
|  | Emancipation | 108 |
| Chapter 4 | Some Highlights From The Field | 110 |
|  | Introduction: | 110 |
|  | Zack | 111 |
|  | Subpoena To Sitka | 113 |
|  | Mint Tea | 116 |
|  | I Steal, You Steal - - - | 118 |
|  | Office Capers | 120 |
|  | Debbie | 123 |
|  | A Shot Hits Home | 126 |
|  | Speaking Of Saints | 127 |
|  | Definitely Not Jackie Chan | 129 |
|  | Not Frank Buck, Either | 131 |
|  | Curly Vi | 134 |
|  | Curly Vii | 136 |
|  | Curly Viii | 137 |

| | | |
|---|---|---|
| Chapter 5 | Jails And Detention | 139 |
| | Introduction: | 139 |
| | Inside | 140 |
| | Some Major Differences | 143 |
| | Why Does Anyone Want To Work There? | 145 |
| | Roaches And Crickets | 147 |
| | Where'd He Go? Where'd He Go? | 155 |
| | Not All Gloom And Doom | 157 |
| | Warriors In Juvenile Detention | 159 |
| | Head Up And Locked Up | 161 |
| | I've Got A Secret | 165 |
| | A Quote To Ponder | 167 |
| | Another Quote | 168 |
| | A Private Prison Story | 170 |
| Chapter 6 | "Homes" Away From Home | 172 |
| | Introduction: | 172 |
| | What Kind Of "Homes?" | 173 |

|  | Gimme Back, My Kid!. . . . . . . . . . . . . 174 |
| --- | --- |
|  | The Naturalist . . . . . . . . . . . . . . . . . . . 179 |
|  | The "Hair Dance" . . . . . . . . . . . . . . . . 184 |
|  | Preventing A Crisis Is Expensive . . . . . 186 |
|  | Whipping Them Into Shape . . . . . . . . 188 |
|  | Boot Camps . . . . . . . . . . . . . . . . . . . . . 195 |
| Chapter 7 | The Academy . . . . . . . . . . . . . . . . . . . 200 |
|  | Introduction: . . . . . . . . . . . . . . . . . . . . 200 |
|  | Creating The Academy . . . . . . . . . . . . 200 |
|  | The Players . . . . . . . . . . . . . . . . . . . . . 204 |
|  | The Pouters . . . . . . . . . . . . . . . . . . . . . 206 |
|  | The Paramedic . . . . . . . . . . . . . . . . . . . 210 |
|  | High Steppin'. . . . . . . . . . . . . . . . . . . . 213 |
|  | Back To The Rez . . . . . . . . . . . . . . . . . 217 |
|  | Spiderman . . . . . . . . . . . . . . . . . . . . . . 220 |
|  | Ram, The Mig Pilot . . . . . . . . . . . . . . 226 |
|  | State Certification . . . . . . . . . . . . . . . . 228 |

Have Academy, Will Travel . . . . . . . . . 231

The Suicide Room . . . . . . . . . . . . . . . . 233

Awards And Rewards . . . . . . . . . . . . . 238

Chapter 8  Retirement . . . . . . . . . . . . . . . . . . . . . . 242

Introduction: . . . . . . . . . . . . . . . . . . . . . 242

Grasshopper, Time For You To Go! . . . 242

Final Rants And Raves . . . . . . . . . . . . 249

Positional Asphyxia . . . . . . . . . . . . . . . 249

Primary Default . . . . . . . . . . . . . . . . . . 252

Honestly. This Is: The Last One . . . . . 255

## *Why Did I Write This Book?*

Actually, I began writing this book for my children and grandchildren. Very early in my career as a Probation Officer I had the opportunity to interview a very old man who had served in the U.S. Army during the 1890s. While this former "Buffalo Soldier," as the Southwestern Indians named the African-American troops, related a number of his experiences I came to realize that Military Generals and Industry Captains do not have an exclusive lock on interesting lives. In fact, I like to think my grandkids will want to say, "Hey, let me tell you about the time granddad watched a 400-pound woman try to shoplift a television set----."

As I progressed through the writing of this book, I came to believe that I could be instrumental in educating citizens in some aspects of the Criminal Justice System not generally explored by television reporters or politicians seeking re-election.

In this book, I will give readers a brief tour of the world of Criminal Justice, as seen through the eyes of this career Probation Officer. We will explore the Probation Officer's place and duties in the Criminal Justice System. We will find that not all the facts in any given case may be found in written reports or court testimony. We will see that in the world of Criminal Justice, there are few black and white situations. And we will come to realize how inane and counterproductive statements such as "Lock 'em up and throw away the key" can be.

While I hope this work will educate, I also hope it will be entertaining. The experiences of Officers in the Criminal Justice System can be, and at times are: tragic, humorous, boring, and heart-pounding. You will discover that I have been exposed to adventures both challenging and gratifying. I promise you that not all criminals are bloodthirsty monsters, and not all officers, attorneys, and judges are exemplary citizens. My colleagues and I behaved neither like television's Sergeant Friday nor like the comic buffoons you saw in "The Pink Panther;" at least not always.

All this notwithstanding, I am mindful of years past in the academic world when I on occasion paid fifty dollars or more for a required book which was clearly a waste of ink and paper. I have done my best to avoid being guilty of this sort of literary travesty. I hope you will find this book an easy and entertaining read.

Finally, I hope this book will motivate you to learn more about how our Criminal Justice System works--- and sometimes works in ways not to our liking, and why. The Criminal Justice System can appear to be complex, confusing, and unsympathetic to victims. The system is foreign to most citizens, and generally is not a primary subject at the dinner table or the workplace; that is unless the citizen has been made a victim of a criminal act.

However, the ordinary citizen can have a positive impact on the Criminal Justice System. I hope this book will encourage you to discover the strengths and weaknesses within your Criminal Justice System -and to work toward improving the system. You will find that you do have the power to make a difference.

For

Shirley, Eric, Alex, Deborah, Carrie, and Patti.
Special thanks to Chuck and Jane Holcombe for their
help in making this adventure readable.

# What Does A Probation Officer Do?

The word "probation" originates from the Latin, "probo," meaning, "prove," or "test," so that a person who is "On Probation" has been convicted of a criminal offense, and, rather than being locked up, the person has been given an opportunity by the Court to "prove" that he or she intends to be a model citizen from that time on.

Well, then, what are the mechanics of "sentencing?"

Simply put, when a person is convicted (found guilty) in a Criminal Court for having committed a criminal offense, that person is subject to penalties. The penalties can include, but not be limited to, incarceration ("lockup"), and/or a monetary penalty (fine).

If a person is found guilty of a Misdemeanor Offense (that is, a "lesser offense"), and is ordered by the Court to be incarcerated, he or she may be sentenced to serve time in a jail, which is a facility usually run by a County, or, as in the State of Louisiana, a "Parrish." In most jurisdictions, the maximum time a person convicted of a Misdemeanor will serve in jail is one year.

If a person is determined by the Court to be guilty of a Felony Offence (a "greater offense") and is ordered by the Court to be incarcerated ("locked up"), he or she will be sent to a prison, which is a secure facility, usually operated by a State Department of Corrections. A person who is incarcerated in a prison can expect to serve no less than one year, and, for some offenses, possibly for his or her entire life, inside those walls.

If a person is convicted of a criminal offense, and the sentencing Judge decides to "suspend" any part of the sentence, that person can be placed on some type of Probation, usually for a set period of time. If the person on Probation violates the Terms Of Probation, the Judge can revoke Probation, and it's "Hello, walls!"

A Probation Officer supervises people who are on Probation. The probation Officer is literally "The Eyes and The Ears" of the sentencing Judge. The Probation Officer supervises the offender and makes certain that the offender follows the rules of probation. These rules often include: Don't break the law. Stay in school (this most often applies in Juvenile or Family Courts) and/or keep a job. Don't leave town without court permission. No Alcohol. No drugs. Pay Child support; et cetera.

Convicted offenders who are on Parole are people who have been convicted of a Felony Offense, have been incarcerated in a State or Federal Prison for some time, and have been released from prison, prior to full completion of the time sentence. These offenders are supervised by a Parole Officer. When someone is placed on Parole, there are behavior rules, or Terms of Parole, similar to the behavior rules for someone who is placed on Probation.

In most cases, Probation Officers are employed by the States' Criminal and Juvenile Courts. Probation

Officers are considered to be "Officers of The Court." Parole Officers are employed by the States' Departments of Corrections.

Probation Officers typically perform other vital functions for the Criminal and the Juvenile Courts. One of the most common functions is Pre- Sentence Investigations and Reports. Commonly, when an offender has been convicted, a Sentencing Hearing will be set on a date, often thirty to ninety days following Conviction. During the interim period, a Probation Officer is assigned to investigate the offender's personal, social and legal history. Those interviewed may include the offender, friends, neighbors, educators, employers, Police Officers, and the victim or the victim's survivors.

The investigating P.O. then creates a Pre-Sentence Report to The Court. The Sentencing Judge uses the information contained in this report as an aid in determining the appropriate sentence for the convicted offender.

As you can see, a Probation Officer's position is incredibly powerful, and it is of supreme importance that the Courts carefully scrutinize applicants for that office. Through their daily contacts with the families, schools, employers, social service agencies, and victims, P.O.'s can greatly enhance, or can utterly destroy, the credibility of a community's Criminal Justice System.

A final note on this subject: for various political and economic reasons, some Probation Departments at the Trial Court (usually called "Superior Court") level are funded, therefore operated, through joint County-state arrangements. Some others may be allocated out to counties, but operated at the State level only. Some Adult and Juvenile Probation Departments are entities separate from each other. Some Juvenile and Adult Probation Departments are merged, and their Probation Officers often handle adults and juveniles on the same caseload. This can be particularly interesting when adults and juveniles in the same family are on Probation.

In some cities and towns, the "Lower Courts," that is, the local County and City level Magistrate and J.P. Courts, employ Probation Officers, who serve only at that level. Finally, in some cities, Police Departments employ their Probation Officers.

There appears to exist conventional wisdom that Probation Officers are primarily desk-bound pencil pushers and bean counters. Indeed, such duties do exist as some, but, thankfully, very few, job assignments in probation departments. I was cursed with this kind of assignment only once, and very briefly. I, at the same time, was never seen wearing a suit. I will admit to wearing a tie and a sports coat, both occasionally matching the rest of my attire, when I went to court because a coat and tie were required for the officers of the court when in court.

Before my final assignment with the department's Detention Division, my duties were primarily on the streets and within my assigned neighborhoods. While on duty my primary mode of transportation was my privately owned motorcycle. My clothing on the streets included slacks, a casual shirt, lace-up boots, and, absolutely, a helmet.

Have I made all this clear? Well, if it's not quite clear, please stay with me anyway. We're going to have a good time!

*Chapter I*

# THE ROOKIE YEARS

## INTRODUCTION:

I enjoy life most when I am given challenges demanding immediate decisions. I also perform best with minimal supervision. For these and other reasons, I felt at home right away when I became a probation officer.

However, I entered into this career not through design, but by happenstance!

This chapter will relate to how I came to be a Probation Officer. I will relate some early on-the-job experiences remaining with me, nearly forty years later, as very vivid memories. I will also introduce a colleague in law enforcement who became a partner and a lifelong friend.

# HOW I BECAME A PROBATION OFFICER

The opportunity of being a P.O. came to me through being at the right place, at the right time.

While completing a Bachelor's Degree, I had secured a part-time position with an agency contracted to the County to provide services to juveniles residing in low-income sections of the city.

The Agency Director was a dynamic man, who took an active interest in his staff. As the Fates would have it, he and I connected right away; I was fascinated by his "war stories" from his former career: he was a retired Chief Probation Officer.

One afternoon "The Chief" called me into his office. There in his office, I met his secretary's husband, who was at the time the County Assistant Chief Probation Officer, later to be Chief of the County Probation Department for twenty years into the future.

"The Chief," said, "Meet Kurt. He ought to be a P.O."

Mr. Assistant Chief said: "Kurt, come talk with me sometime."

Had that invitation been offered only one year earlier, I would have, at that meeting, essentially experienced the entire hiring process for a P.O., before 1968. The only further requirement would have been an affirmation of my hire by the Presiding Judge. That's right: until 1968, in my State, this was all that was required to fill this incredibly powerful position within the Criminal Justice

System. All else you needed was a clean legal record and a Friendly Nod of the Head from the Presiding Judge.

However, by 1968, the era of Judicial appointments of P.O.'s was brought to a halt by the State Legislature: now required was: A Bachelor's Degree, preferably in a field related to the requirements of performing a P.O.'s job, successful completion of a written examination and also two interviews.

Came 1969 and, having completed my B.A., I successfully met these aforementioned employment requirements, and was therefore duly appointed to enter into what was to become my thirty-two-year career.

The term "Rookie" does not necessarily, by itself, humble a Rookie. I have known few rookie Probation Officers, myself included, who did not truly believe, deep down in their heart of hearts, that they had come into the job with all "the answers." This phenomenon arises partly through the pride of attaining this new, Exalted Status, and partly through the effect of four years of exposure to the Ivory Tower of education in a University. For all my education and life experience, in 1969 I found I was not yet really endowed with a full understanding of "criminal thought process," "dysfunctional family dynamics" or "how works the Courts and Corrections Systems."

I am certain that my lack of criminal savvy would have come as a surprise to my childhood teachers and counselors, some of whom, I have discovered in recent years, had believed that I'd died either in prison or by a Police Officer's firearm. By my age 17 I was a school dropout, and, by virtue of my mother's ability to work faster than a Juvenile Court Judge, I was introduced into the event-filled life of a United States Marine, commencing in sunny San Diego, California.

Eight years later, after having been provided the opportunity to help keep the world safe from Communism, I re-entered civilian life, armed with some college education, and with a license to fly airplanes. However, old reputations die hard, and many of the folks who had "known me when" were unprepared to recognize the shiny and wonderful "New Me".

I married a young lady who liked Marines. We moved to Cordova City, Where I attended the State University (Sociology Major) and, ultimately, became a Probation Officer; one of the very Species that had been scowling and shouting at me, only a little over ten years earlier.

On the morning of my first day as a Probation Officer, I was presented with an office and a Field Caseload. Shortly after lunch, I was introduced to my Supervisor. The Supervisor spent the next several days reviewing with me my one-hundred-plus Field Probation Cases, and my twenty-plus Pre- Sentence Investigation cases, all pending Sentencing Hearings. He told me that for the next thirty days I was to present to him, first thing each morning, my day's work plan and any pre-sentence reports I may have written.

I was told that the easiest way to meet the people on my Caseload was to "Cite them in:" send a letter to each Probationer, directing them to appear at my office at an appointed date and time. It was during these meetings that this neophyte P.O. discovered that, contrary to conventional wisdom, offenders are neither "Black" nor "White," in terms of race, economic lifestyles, or social backgrounds. For the most part, I sensed no hostility nor reserve from my "clients;" rather, many Probationers went out of their way to help the Rookie to understand how the Justice System worked with them and what they hoped the outcome of the Probation experience would be. I also discovered that with a Juvenile case, the parents usually saw themselves as being on Probation as well.

The Pre-Sentence Investigation cases were another species entirely. To investigate the legal, social, and personal backgrounds of individuals, and to interview victims, I needed to be face-to-face with the people, and on their turf, not mine. This meant that my old '63 Bug was to become familiar with a lot of Cordova City pavement, and through my travels, I came to possess a file cabinet full of contacts in the world of business, education, social services, and street informants so that in the future a few telephone calls would save me many hours and many miles of travel time.

My Supervisor's 30-day theory was accurate: by the end of that time, I at least had a fair grasp of what I was supposed to do. But it would still be a long time before I knew how best to meet my responsibilities.

# THE POWDER BLUE NEGLIGEE

As was typical of Juvenile Delinquents' Probation files during the Sixties, Ross Billings' file was several inches thick. Ross had been cited by the Police and referred to the Juvenile Court not less than twenty-six times.

This lad had been placed on Probation/continued on Probation five times over three years. He had been a guest of our Detention Facility twelve times. This time, the Police informed me, he had dropped sugar down the school principal's gas tank.

When I met Ross at the Detention Facility entrance, he expressed a certain amount of disdain toward the school staff and also toward the Police, who clearly could not take a joke.

A few hours' studies through the Probation File of the rehabilitation efforts directed toward Ross showed that he had enjoyed the therapeutic efforts of a number of child and family psychologists and counselors. He had been transferred over several years to every Junior High School and High School in the school District. He'd been on a Psychotropic Drug Regimen, courtesy of prescriptions written by the family Psychiatrist over the past two years. Unhappily, he did not appear to be particularly appreciative of everyone's efforts to improve his future.

Finding all this to be a bit overwhelming to my Rookie mind, I consulted my Supervisor. I handed the file to him. He saw the name, "Ross Billings," and scowled. His observation: "I strongly suggest that you recommend (to the Sentencing Judge) that this kid be sent to the State Department of Juvenile Corrections."

In those days, that would have meant a commitment to a particular Juvenile Corrections Facility which several years later was transformed into a minimum-security Adult Prison. This facility had a mean, some would say brutal, reputation of being a Spartan and corporal punishment-oriented correction facility. Located on the site of an actual Nineteenth Century

"Indian Wars" U.S. Army fort, was placed in an area where the terrain was flat and even the cactus had difficulty surviving. Inmates of this prison rarely referred to the Warden of the prison of some thirty years by name,

but only as "That Bastard." Juveniles in trouble with the law, myself included in the Fifties, would generally come to tears and resort to pleading when threatened with incarceration into this place. Juvenile Parolees from that Prison were generally given wide berth by all but the toughest thugs.

So it came to pass that I informed Mr. And Mrs. Billings that I would be asking the sentencing judge to order commitment to this State facility for young Ross Billings. The parents were, understandingly, quite upset.

Mr. And Mrs. Billings were employed as professional fashion models. Both looked like "Bay Watch" stars. Neither, according to my file, had finished High School. Their general lack of understanding of their son's behavior and the Juvenile Justice System reflected folks whose universe revolved around themselves. They were Masters of the Excuse. They correctly identified me as a newcomer to the game, so they directed every effort toward blaming the schools, the counselors, the courts, and, of course, the cops and P.O.'s for their son's misguided behavior. They were the first of thousands who would say to me: "I know my child, and my child would never...."

While they complained, I thought of my own three encounters with young Ross during the weeks preceding his most current arrest and detention: twice I'd gone in the morning to his home, literally dragged him out of bed, then sent him off to school. On a Saturday I'd personally escorted him to a barbershop for a haircut so the school principal would allow him back in. I was developing a genuine sympathy for social workers.

I carried Mr. And Mrs. Billings complaints to my Supervisor the next morning. His reply: "Commitment to the State." And, of course, he was right.

Sentencing for young Ross Billings was set for a Friday morning. During Monday afternoon of that week, I received a telephone call from Mrs. Billings. She sounded very emotional and tearful; she wanted me to meet with her and her husband the following morning in a last-ditch effort to explore options other than to the State for their son. I agreed to meet with them at their home, at 7:30 A.M.

On Tuesday morning, I drove to their home and parked along the curb: this is a practice I'd picked up from some of the Department veterans: Parking in a residential driveway makes one's car vulnerable to being blocked and trapped. I exited my "63 VW Bug and proceeded along the sidewalk to the front door...the door opened. Mrs. Billings was standing there.

She was, as usual, incredibly beautiful. She was wearing a very skimpy, very filmy, powder blue negligee. She smiled and said: "come on in!"

Yes, I was married; yes, I was nearly 30 years old; and yes, my senses were screaming: "Setup! Setup!" I said: "I 'm sorry, I must have arrived too early. I'll go out and grab a cup of coffee and be back in a half-hour."

Mrs. Billing's smile dropped. She closed the front door as I entered my "63 Bug. I closed the driver's side door, started the engine, and ….

Mr. Billing's car raced past me and onto his driveway.

Mr. Billings jumped out of his car and raced up to, then through, the front door of his house, shouting: "Take your hands off my wife, you Son…"

As I drove toward the nearest pay telephone, I came to fully understand what the Billings' had planned. At Ross Billing's Sentencing Hearing his parents would have said: "Judge, instead of helping our child, this lecherous Probation Officer was making unwanted sexual advances on the child's mother!" Ross Billings would then be freed, and the Probation Officer would be fired.

I immediately called my Supervisor. He chuckled and told me to return to the Department right away and write a report of this incident for the Judge.

On Friday morning we all appeared in the Courtroom of the Presiding Judge. His Honor heard Counsels' arguments and promptly dispatched young Ross Billings to the State Department of Corrections.

Twenty-five years later I was to be given charge of the Juvenile Detention Officers Academy. I never failed to spin this tale to each new Class of Rookies. The Uninitiated have no idea as to how devious- and seductive- offenders and their families can be.

# THE RUBBER STAMP

Every legal document is important. Every legal document will have an impact to some measure on someone's life.

I have developed an opinion that some legal work, particularly clerical work, becomes so routine that it can easily be forgotten that people's lives are impacted every time we open and close a file drawer. And when one's "In" basket is stacked with what appears to be job security for the next two years, the mind can become numb. The goal becomes one of making the "In" stack smaller. We gather the papers; we disperse the papers.

One such routine function during the early years was to summarily release from probation those juveniles who had been "successful," e.g., appeared, at least, to have followed all the rules for one year, or who had, in any event, achieved the twenty-first birthday.

Although a Rookie, even I could not believe the abysmal state of my new Caseload. There were persons on Juvenile Probation who were well over twenty-one years of age and not yet released. I discovered one such fellow had been convicted as an Adult and was residing in a Prison. Some offenders had not been checked upon for months. Other offenders swore they had not seen their

P.O. for months, although the contact log in the file was current. "Report and Reviews," always to be read and signed by a Judge, were not current. A few Misdemeanant offenders had been on Probation for several years, not further offended, and still not released from Probation.

What I did not understand at the time was that the weight of the number of these Caseloads was often so overwhelming that the assigned Officers could hardly do more than the absolute minimal Court-required casework, then "Wave a Magic Wand" over the rest. Officer turnover was rampant: except for the veteran Officers, it seemed that there was a nearly complete rookie turnover every six months or less. Most, I believe, resigned over frustration.

Some were frustrated because of the size of the workload. Some left because they were incapable of functioning without intensive supervision. Some left because they could not handle the emotional impact that is inevitable when directly affecting others' lives in the Criminal Justice System. Consequently, some Caseloads were left unsupervised for six months and longer.

In short, during the early 1970s, the Probation Department simply did not have sufficient resources to hire, fully train and adequately compensate its Probation Officers. Additionally, there needed to be a significant increase in hiring and training new Probation Officers to bring the size of the Caseloads down to a manageable number. When, in the mid-1970s, a new Chief Probation Officer was installed (the same Assistant Chief I'd met a few years earlier), the Department and its resources took a dramatic change for the better.

When I told my Supervisor of the shape of my Caseload, he suggested that I write out a sort of "blanket" Court Order, wherein I would recommend a release from Probation for a long list of people. He did mention that upon the release of those people from Probation, there would be an equal number of new cases assigned to me to replace them.

I carefully wrote out the Order, with my recommendation for release, of those long overdue for release. Having now actually written out this document, I was somewhat taken aback by the length of the list of names.

I carried the completed document to the chambers of the appropriate Judge. The man was seated behind his desk, conferring with his clerk. Both looked up at me and smiled. The Judge asked, "Yes?"

"Uh, Your Honor, I have a list of people on this Document, who, per my Supervisor, need to be released from Probation."

"Give me the Document."

I handed the document to His Honor. He looked at it and for a short time, then, scowling, looked up at me and asked:

"So, your Supervisor sent you?"

"Yes, Your Honor."

"And these people need to be released?" "Yes, Your Honor."

"And your Supervisor approves?" "Yes, Your Honor."

"So where the hell is your Supervisor's signature on this Document?"

Omigod. I had forgotten to go to the Supervisor for his review and signature! I know I visibly slumped.

His Honor, now the King of Scowls, shouted:

"Don't you ever again bring ANYTHING to me without your Supervisor's, signature." What do you think I am-YOUR RUBBER STAMP??!! Now get out of here and go see your Supervisor!"

I double-timed out of his chambers and hurried forthwith to my Supervisor's office. When I entered, he informed me that he had already received a call from the Judge. He perused my release document, signed it, and sent me back to see His Honor.

I knocked on His Honor's door. A voice growled, "Come in." I entered. "Well, are you here for me to RUBBER STAMP another one of your documents?"

"Uh, no, Your Honor, I'm back from my Supervisor's office with his signature on the release form."

His Honor snatched the document from my hand, glanced at it, set it aside, and said: "Get Out."

I was only too happy to leave. Lesson learned!!

Several days later, the Judge's clerk told me that His Honor and my Supervisor had enjoyed long and hearty laughter over how they had taught the Rookie proper protocol.

Footnote: This Judge was a much-admired man from a local family of Physicians and Attorneys, which had settled here generations ago. Shortly after this incident, I discovered that, like myself, he was an avid history buff. He and I soon became good friends.

# BABY DUCKS

Budget and staffing woes notwithstanding, the Probation Department in the early '70s did make an honest attempt to bring training to the Officers. A number of psychologists and at least two psychiatrists visited on occasion to provide classes in issues around family dysfunction and intervention, schizophrenia, alcoholism, and so forth; mostly, very excellent classes.

However, during one training class the instructor, a family therapist, was emphasizing that Officers need to realize that we must be objective and open-minded when judging human behavior. She wanted us to realize that issues around "sick" and "normal" behavior must be addressed cautiously; that we must not "jump to conclusions."

"For example," she said, "when I was a little girl I once gathered up some baby ducks, then I buried them up to their necks, and then I ran a lawnmower over them. Now, who can say that was sick?"

No one said a word. My God, this woman was working with children!

# HAPPY NEW YEAR

Johnny Moore was a tall, muscular, seventeen-year-old Black kid whose wide, toothy grin seemed to never go away. The son of a sharecropping family south of Cordova City, Johnny had barely graduated from the eighth grade. A Psychological evaluated his intelligence as "dull-normal". He was an affable, easy-going young man. He loved to joke around and always addressed me, even in Court, as "Nee Mann."

Johnny loved cars. He never owned a car, nor did he possess a driver's license. Nevertheless, on a number of occasions Police Officers would discover him behind the wheel of someone's car. Of course, it was always without "someone's" knowledge or consent.

It was never shown that Johnny ever actually stole a car. He would "obtain" them usually from car thieves who either tired of the car or believed the car was too "hot" to continue to drive. Johnny didn't seem to mind about the car's history, he just wanted to drive.

Johnny was on Probation, and my Probation Caseload.

During the autumn of 1970, Johnny began to disappear from home and farm for several days at a time. His mother would call me each time and after several such disappearances and reappearances I finally confronted Johnny at his home. When I inquired as to his whereabouts and activities while gone he gave me his usual side grin and said:

"Shit, Nee Mann, ain't no need for you to get mad, I didn't do no dope or nothing."

Okay, no problem, he was just "out somewhere" with "friends." His mother and I were worried, but Johnny saw "no problem."

How many hundreds of times have I heard a parent or a counselor say to one of my probationers, "Well if Billy jumped off a bridge would you jump too?" In fact, in the cases of large numbers of my probationers, they would jump, too. Johnny Moore was one of those kids.

It came to pass that during early December 1970, a very intoxicated Johnny Moore was arrested and detained. The following morning, a very sick and tearful Johnny sat in the holding cell and told me he could not remember where he had been, that he had been with "just a bunch an Indians with cases of beer." It did come to pass that the highway patrol found him lying, passed out, in the middle of a highway, at 2 A.M.

Johnny had a long history with the Juvenile Justice System and it was clear at his arraignment hearing that the system had come to the end of the line with him. The Court ordered that he remain a resident in our Detention Facility. His sentencing was set for mid-January, 1971. I did not doubt as to what the Judge expected me to recommend: commitment to the State Department of Corrections. Johnny and his parents appeared to accept the young man's likely fate at sentencing as inevitable.

When each morning through December 1970 I visited Johnny, he was in good spirits. He seemed to have no grasp as to what his likely living conditions were to be from January 1971 and probably up to his twenty-first birthday. He had his "three shots and a cot," and he was happy.

New Year's Eve, 1970 was one of those holidays when I should have gone out, partied, and spent overnight at a friend's house. However, I did not.

For reasons I do not recall, I read, drank a few tumblers of scotch on the rocks, and went to bed. Then, shortly after Midnight at 1 A.M., January 1st, 1971, I was wide-awake, dressed, and driving in my '63 Bug to the Juvenile Detention Facility.

I had been awakened by my telephone, which was, I knew right away, heralding Bad News (have you ever received Good News from a middle-of-the-night call?). The familiar voice of my first Supervisor, now the Department's new Assistant Chief, cheerily bade me a good morning, then told me:

"You have to come down to Juvenile Detention!" I replied, "well, Happy New Year to you, too,"

"No kidding, Kurt, Johnny Moore is your kid, right?" "Yes, so…?"

"He's one of the ringleaders in a riot down there. The inmates have both cellblocks barricaded. They've started some fires. You have to go down there and talk to Johnny."

Would a veteran Juvenile Probation Officer reply to the Assistant Chief, "Oh hell yes, I'll be right down there and jump right into the middle of a Detention riot at 1 A.M.?" Gimme a break! However, I was no veteran P.O.;

I was a Rookie who, only a short time earlier, had been a Marine, following orders without question in the field. So, "Semper Fi," I went to the Juvenile Detention Facility.

At 1:30 A.M., I drove into the Detention Facility parking lot. It appeared to also be the official parking lot for the Sheriff's Office, the Cordova City Police, and the State Troopers. I exited my Bug, walked past a platoon of officers wearing riot gear, and greeted the man who had awakened me and asked me to join the party.

The Assistant Chief said: "Okay, Kurt, here's the deal: The inmates have calmed down a little, but all the cellblock lights are out and there's some stuff on fire. The cellblocks are barricaded. We need you to go in there and bring Johnny Moore out."

I replied "See you in a little bit," and entered the Detention Facility through the steel main doors. Just like that. Not a thought in my mind. Not a brain in my head.

The Detention Facility had been built during the Great Depression. It was square and, like the 19th-century forts you see in Indian war movies, the center was an open area (it was called "the patio"). Cellblock one was Located along the East wall. Cellblock two was along the South wall. The mess area and Nurses' office were together (conveniently?) on the West wall, and the North wall contained administrative offices and the holding cell. On the roof, all the way around the Facility was a six-foot chain-link fence topped with barbed wire.

I walked from the Northside, across "The Patio", toward the entrance to the cellblock, which on the outside made up the East wall. I could see a few small fires and there was a stench that would make a Rhino gag. There, at the doorway, barricaded by mattresses, stood Johnny Moore, a huge grin on his face. Johnny shouted:

"Hey, Nee Mann, Happy New Year!"

At this time, all the other inmates were silent. They were watching me. I imagined they were thinking," What kind of idiot would come in here without a gun and a cop escort?

The cellblock appeared as though it had been bombed. All the beds were overturned, the plumbing ripped out, everything electrical torn out of the ceiling and off the walls.

I said, "Johnny, you have to come with me." Johnny replied, "Okay."

He climbed over the mattress barricade and walked out to the Patio to join me. Together we walked through the main doors out to the parking lot, where Sheriff's Deputies immediately took custody of Johnny.

I at last began to realize where I had just gone and what I had just done. Sometimes I wonder what has kept me alive.

I never saw Johnny again. My Department never made any further mention of the incident to me. I would guess that had there been an official mention made, it would have been like a Certificate, citing me as "Dumbass Rookie of the Year."

# THE SICK IN

The Detention Facility was reconditioned following the New Year riot, to be no more in disarray and unsafe as it was originally; and it was reoccupied in quick order. It had been, from its opening, rundown, unsafe for inmates and staff and great fun for inmates to escape from. More on that later!

At any given time, the old Juvenile Detention Facility (now long since torn down and replaced) housed no less than 150 boys over age 12, several dozen "junior boys" aged 8-12 and, in a separate building, joined to the "Boys Section" by a chain link and barbed wire passageway, fifty-plus girls.

During any shift, a staff consisting of no more than four men and three women were responsible for the "care, custody and control" of two-hundred-plus juvenile offenders. A nurse was on duty for several hours, a few days per week. Medications were passed out to the juveniles by Detention Officers.

The qualifications for Juvenile Detention Officers, up to the mid-1970s, were: High School graduate and no criminal record. The training was: "Here's a Key. Watch how the other stuff works."

The dispensing of medication by Juvenile Detention Officers had been a smoldering ember of contention for years. Officers claimed, correctly, that they were unqualified and untrained for such duty; they wanted medical personnel to be responsible for this.

Juvenile Detention Officers had a long list of very valid grievances, most addressing the Officer-to-inmate ratio. The Detention Officers were the stepchildren of the system; always short of everything, especially training.

Shortly following the reentry of the newly "refurbished" Facility, the Detention Officers, believing they had been "stonewalled" by the Court and Probation Administrators long enough, decided to hold a "Sick In."

In order to be visible to any who might care, this "Sick in" was performed by Detention Officers forming a "Picket" line, complete with "Sick in" signs, along the outside wall of the offices of the Presiding Judge and the Probation Department Chief.

The Presiding Judge fired them all immediately and ordered that the Probation Department fill the void with Probation Officers.

Thus, Probation Officers came to provide the majority of the staffing of the Juvenile Detention Facilities; a condition lasting through the 1990s. The Adult Detention Facilities continued to be operated by Sheriff's Deputies and Sheriff's Detention Officers.

Staffing our Juvenile Detention Facilities thereby became far more expensive, but the inmate-to-staff ratio quickly dropped to one Officer per every ten inmates. And every "Detention Officer," is a Probation Officer, now possessed a college degree.

Full-time nursing staff was created from the ranks of the County Health Department. Nurses dispensed medication; our Officers were forbidden to have anything to do with the medications. In the end, then, it meant that the "Sick-In" participants did create positive change for the Juvenile Detention environment; however, for them, the change was not so positive.

# LET'S GO OUT FOR LUNCH

You may recall that our old Detention Facility, that fun place where Johnny Moore and I celebrated New Year, 1971, was built in the shape of a square, and with a large, open, "Patio" area in the center. Yes, the roof, all the way around, was topped with a chain-link fence and barbed wire.

On the Patio, during any given day, there would be no less than eighty teenaged offenders milling around. The only real physical activity they were allowed was to dribble basketballs. Detention rules were that these inmates were not to be allowed to go near the walls: the walls could be easily scaled and, once on the roof, a brave, or foolhardy, an inmate could climb the fence, go over the barbed wire, jump off the roof and dash into the cotton fields surrounding the Detention Facility.

At the same time, rarely would there be more than three Detention Officers "maintaining order" on the patio.

For decades, a weekly time-honored game would be played by juvenile inmates: one group of inmates staged a "fight" on one side of the patio, causing Officers to intervene; another group of inmates would boost one, two, or more fellow inmates up the opposite sidewall to freedom.

Most escapees were apprehended, usually in very short order. This behavior became sufficiently routine that it was expected. The Sheriff's Department at the time had created a special unit, whose daily function was to lie in waiting for juvenile escapees.

At nearly noon one day, a particular stalwart escapee made his way over the wall. Due to his experience as a juvenile delinquent, he expected no problem in hotwiring a car in the parking lot and making his flight in style. He chose a car and went to work.

As he was making ready the prospective escape car's ignition, he was approached by a gentleman who asked the youth what he was doing?

"I'm trying to get my car started," the youth replied.

"Ah, but this is MY car, said the Probation Department Chief.

## GIMME MY GIRLFRIEND!

This will be yet one more tale about the old Juvenile Detention facility of my Rookie years.

The boyfriend of a detained young lady deeply resented this intervention into his love life by the Court and he was determined to secure her release. He and his companions developed what they believed to be a foolproof, if not outright heroic, plan.

The Girl's Section of the old Juvenile Detention Facility consisted of a rectangular building, set apart from the Boys' building, and connected to the Boys building by a chain link and barbed wired "tunnel" walkway. A further chain link and barbed wired fence surrounded the Girl's Section.

The girls were allowed at times to go outside the building, to mill about inside the fenced areas, whenever a female Detention Officer could be spared to supervise. There generally is a one Officer-to-thirty-or-more girl's ratio, supervision was of course problematic. It was therefore relatively easy to smuggle the boyfriend's written escape plan to the detained girl through the perimeter fence.

The escape plan was extensively thought out. On a particular night, the boyfriend and his companions would go to the Detention Facility perimeter fence and toss Molotov Cocktails at the Girls Detention building. Detention Officers, upon seeing the resulting conflagration, would immediately evacuate the girls to the outside area. The detained girlfriend would then exit the grounds through a hole cut in the chain-link fence by the boyfriend. Steve McQueen would be proud!

On the assigned night, the young rescuers arrived at the Girls Detention Facility perimeter fence.

The Boyfriend lit and threw a Molotov Cocktail over the fence. The cocktail fell short into some bushes and fizzled out.

The boyfriend lit and threw a second Molotov Cocktail. While in the air, the lit rag departed the bottle. No fire there!

The boyfriend lit and threw a third Molotov Cocktail. This one struck the steel Girls Detention Building entrance door, and then bounced onto the concrete sidewalk; the bottle shattered: there was heard a "whoosh!" Fire at last!!

The fire burning on the sidewalk quickly ran out of fuel and went out in less than a minute. No Detention staff seemed to notice.

Exasperated, the boyfriend determined that he would enter the Detention Facility himself, and personally retrieve his girlfriend. He entered the grounds through the hole he'd cut into the fence. He ran to the Girls Detention building door and pounded.

A voice from a loudspeaker said "Yes?"

The boyfriend shouted:" Let me in, I have a gun!" The electrically operated steel door clicked open. The boyfriend entered the building.

The Electrically operated door clicked shut behind him!

# LARRY

It was one of those rare Cordova City winter afternoons where the sky was not only overcast; we also had rain. I was on my way out of my office to go home. The phone rang, and of course, Rookie that I was, I answered it.

It was Detention. The voice on the other end snarled "Lucky You! You're the only Probation Officer still here and the cops have brought in an INKY"

An "INKY" is an "Incorrigible Child." "Incorrigibility" is not a "Criminal" act, nor is it a "Delinquent" act; it is a "Status Offence." In other words, if the accused is a minor, he can be charged. If he's an adult, he cannot be charged.  (Confused? Don't worry, there's more about this in Chapter Three.) Since I'd not yet learned to leave the Department grounds as soon as possible each day, clearly this "INKY" case was to fall to me. I walked over to Juvenile Detention.

Larry Bon was sitting on a bench in the holding cell. His mother and two Cordova City Police Officers were waiting for me. Once the Police Officers were satisfied that I had the case well in hand, they departed.

Jenny Bon, Larry's mother, was a petite, frail appearing woman of 35 years. Her 16-year old son was huge-easily six feet tall and a very bulky 200 plus pounds. "He hit me," Jenny said, then, burst into tears. "He hits me all the time, especially when he's drunk. He throws my furniture around. He's put

chairs through my windows and tonight he beat holes in my walls with the telephone." "He beats on his girlfriend, too."

Jenny Bon had called the Police during the outburst of that afternoon and asked that Larry be detained as a very Incorrigible, out-of-control youth. Larry was drunk and angry and the Police had the very Devil to pay, finally after a struggle, handcuffing Larry and getting him into the patrol car.

Now, Larry was quiet and subdued. I entered the holding cell and sat on the bench next to him. There were tears in his eyes. I could smell the booze on this breath. Larry would not respond to my questions beyond an occasional grunt. It was clear that he was going to be with us at least until after his first court appearance. I asked the Detention Officers to book Larry in, and then I returned to where his mother was sitting.

It took very little effort on my part to obtain from Jenny Bon a pertinent family history: of French-Canadian origin, Jenny had, at the time of this interview, been married a total of seven times. Her first husband was a Canadian police officer. Jenny said she married this man,

Larry's father, because he reminded her of her father. They divorced soon after Larry was born. The man, she said was a violent alcoholic.

During our discussion, Jenny said that she remembered one night when, as a child, she watched her parents fight. Her father doused her mother's head with some sort of liquid then set her hair afire. Jenny then began a description of her second, also alcoholic, husband. Yes, it seems that she met all her future husbands at "pubs." In fact, at one point during this interview, she looked at me directly in the eyes and said: "I just don't understand how come every man I marry is a drunk who beats me."

It was now clear what the story was going to be on all seven husbands. I decided to save further information gathering for a later date. I did offer Court-financed family therapy sessions for her and Larry, which she gratefully accepted. I did not, however, delude myself into thinking this would be the family's first, or last, an excursion into counseling.

I sent Jenny Bon home, spoke briefly with Larry once again, and then sent myself home. It was still raining, only now the sky was black. This was my Very First "INKY" case, and, yes, I was thoroughly depressed.

Larry was adjudicated ("Found Guilty") as an Incorrigible Child, and placed on Probation, and my Caseload. During the year he was on my Caseload, he stayed in counseling and kept his emotions in check. I helped him join a 12-Step Program. He finished High School with my G.E.D., and when he turned eighteen, he left home. I never heard of Larry again.

By the time we released Larry from Probation, his mother Jenny had been married, and divorced, a total of nine times.

# HOUDINI

The lesson I learned, in this case, was: "watch what you say, and how you say it."

The juvenile, in this case, was a fifteen-year-old boy. He had a very pale complexion and bright red hair. He was a chronic runaway, so it is no wonder that I rarely saw him and never really got to know him.

His runaway patter was clear: He'd ditch school, usually on a Friday, and run away to San Diego, California with his adult, homosexual, lover. After a week or two, he'd be apprehended. His father would drive to San Diego and retrieve his son from the San Diego County Juvenile authorities.

As far as I know, the adult lover was never apprehended or prosecuted.

Following one of the runaways and return from San Diego, the dad called me and wanted advice. "How can I keep him home? I've tried locking him in his room, but he just goes out the window."

In what was one of my least intelligent moments, I replied, "I dunno, maybe you ought to chain him to his bed."

Several days later, the dad called again: "Mr. Nee Mann, I did what you said; I chained him to his bed, but he picked the lock and went out the window again."

# PAINTER

It has been my experience that the Courts have never been fully capable of adequately coping, particularly financially, with psychiatric cases. In-house treatment costs are astronomical. When I retired in 2001, psychiatric hospitalization of a juvenile could be expected to cost $25,000 monthly – just for bed and board. Psychotropic drugs were extra. How many cases at this rate can the taxpayers be expected to finance on an annual basis? As advanced and resourceful as my own Probation Department had become well before I retired, we never had a prayer of adequately meeting the community's needs for Court-ordered hospitalization and treatment of psychiatric cases.

During the early 1970s, this situation was hopeless. As many readers pass through the stories I have entered herein, some may wonder why I, like a P.O., did not make more efforts toward psychiatric interventions for people who were in need. The answer is economics. The fact is, the Courts' budgets for meaningful psychiatric interventions have never been adequate.

Extremely depressed, or extremely dangerous, persons residing in our Juvenile Detention Facility during the '70s were often "isolated," in individual cells, entirely walled with tempered glass. This made it possible for observation of up to one dozen "isolated" inmates by one Detention Officer. On occasion, one of those "isolated" persons would be mine.

Ollie Painter was one of my more depressed, occasionally suicidal, charges. To my memory he never was charged with a Delinquent (Criminal) act; He was just another "INKY" who would at times raise hell at home, then fall into a deep depression. His arms and legs were replete with scars from razor cuts.

I received word that Ollie was in detention again and that he was in our front isolation cell, more or less on a "Suicide Watch." Ollie's Public Defender was trying to contact me; it was time to make yet one more impassioned plea to the Court for psychiatric hospitalization for Ollie. I called Ollie's lawyer and told him I would get to work on setting up a hospital bed as soon as I got back from the Juvenile Detention Facility.

When I went into the isolation section, a surreal scene was before me: Ollie Painter was painting the cell walls, slowly and meticulously, with his feces! Of course, the stench was beyond belief. As one might suppose, Detention Officers were very reluctant to intervene, but at length, they had no choice. Their efforts at the cleanup of Ollie and the cell were heroic.

This was one of those events that have remained with me as starkly as though I had seen it yesterday.

Of course, the Court ordered Ollie hospitalized "for observation". Of course, when the money ran out (72 hours) he was released, complete with a grand, economically impossible, set of psychiatric diagnoses, prescriptions, and other observations and recommendations.

Two weeks later Ollie Painter was dead. It came as no surprise that he was a suicide.

## F.Y.V.M.

The early Seventies featured the Hippie Era, the time of the Flower Children, Free Love, and lots of Marijuana. Drugs were rampant and beyond control. Literature abounded at the time regarding the sad and hopeless state of America's Youth (Those folks who, today, are our now-adult educators, politicians, executives, lawyers, and prisoners) going to hell in a hand-basket due to the influence of insane music, Godlessness, and drugs, particularly that Evil Weed, Cannabis (Marijuana).

I was far more strongly convinced then than I am today that the doomsayers were right regarding Marijuana. However, at that time, I was a Hawk-On-Drugs Probation Officer, and I was in fine company: Police, Prosecutors, Judges jumped on Criminal cases involving Marijuana without hesitation. Probation caseloads and jails were overflowing with Marijuana adjudications (convictions).

It was a practice at the time that, when a Probationer had been released by the Court from Probation, a Probation Officer/Probationer office conference would be scheduled. There, the newly released former probationer would be handed his Court Order of release and his P.O.'s congratulations. I had scheduled just such a meeting with an eighteen-year-old male Marijuana probationer.

Although this particular young man had maintained his belief that Marijuana was harmless, he had nevertheless not been further arrested or otherwise been held to violate Probation. Regardless, I had determined that it would be in his best interest for me to provide him with one final lecture regarding the use of the Evil Weed at this release conference.

By this time our Probation Department was growing---at last---at such a pace that individual Officer's offices were no longer possible. Hence, the scheduled conference would be attended as well by my office mate, one Rookie, named Ed Jankins. Ed was up to it: A very good-humored, sharp-witted young man (he later married into money and became a bank executive), he was both an informative and entertaining partner. He had never, at that time, witnessed one of these release conferences, so this experience would count as training for him as well.

At the appointed time, there was a knock on the office door and enter my soon-to-be-former probationer. I bade him draw up a chair and be comfortable before my desk.

I handed the Court's Probation Release Document to the young man, congratulated him, and then launched into what I knew was an eloquent argument against Marijuana use. I asked my former probationer if he had any questions; He responded in the negative, and I formally dismissed this youth from the care, custody, and control of the Juvenile Court.

The young man stood up, replaced his chair along the office wall, walked to the door, grinned, and said: "Mr. Nee Mann, Fuck You Very Much!"

Then, he departed.

I stood, shocked in my disbelief. Ed Jenkins fell out of his chair, Laughing.

## "CURLY"

Edmundo "Curly" Melendez, Cordova City Police Officer, now retired, is a native son of Cordova City. When Curly was a kid, Anglos openly held Hispanics in very low esteem: the term, Wetback" was used openly and often. Hispanic kids were severely punished by public school staff, and by other authority figures as well, for speaking Spanish. During the early 1950s my Hispanic neighbors never admitted to being "Mexican," but uniformly alluded to "Spanish" ancestry. Anglo attitudes toward Hispanics – and vice versa – of that time are accurately portrayed in that era's "West Side Story." To this day, I do not recall hearing Curly speak more than a few dozen sentences in Spanish, and then only when we were dealing with Hispanic gangbangers.

Curly is approximately five feet eight inches tall, and, when younger, had a large mass of thick curly hair on his head, hence the nickname was given him early on by our "clientele." I believe most people would describe him as quiet and unassuming; however, he can become quite animated when around his close friends, or when he is physically attacked. When on the job, his assessments of people have been both incisive and accurate.

Because he is a "Minority," Curly could have been hired by the Cordova City Police Department with no testing---they offered a kind of No Hassle, Instant Employment Program for Minorities---much to the dismay of many of the then existing cops---but he decided instead to go the long, normal, employment route. He doesn't like "special treatment," and he tends to resent people who take it. He says "Getting In Free" is demeaning.

Curly became a Police Officer three years after I joined the Probation Department. Since not all his experiences also included me, for which I was at times very grateful, I have chosen to include within this book's chapters some of his recollections in his own words. What follows are a few of his experiences, in his words, regarding his training as a rookie Police Officer:

## CURLY I: ROOKIE COP

My Rookie time would not be viewed as Politically Correct training in this day and age. When I joined the Police Department, I was sworn in and given a gun and a Badge on my first day of employment. I was assigned to the Identification Bureau, where I spent approximately 30 days, stapling supplemental reports to original crime reports. I was instructed by one Supervisor not to read the reports. I was told by another Supervisor, to read the reports, it would be a good way to learn how to write them.

This was the first of many "Catch-22" problems during my 23 years as a Cop.

The Police Academy lasted 16 weeks. About two weeks into the training, while in Morning Formation, the guy to my right whispered to me, "Look behind you". I turned my head to look. The guy behind me had his loaded .357 magnum handgun pointed right at me. I told the guy to put it back in his holster or I was going to shove it up to his ass. The Sergeant approached and started yelling at me for talking in formation, and would not let me tell him why I did. I was told to run "Discipline Hill" for talking information. The officer with the wayward handgun was fired 2 days later. I guess that someone told the Sergeant what had happened. That was a "Catch-357" problem!

I have studied Martial Arts from age of 16. One day at the Academy, we were being instructed on how to strike with the use of a baton. I opened my big mouth and asked the Instructor if it wouldn't be more effective to use a circular motion, rather than a straight arm swing. The Instructor related he would think about it. Well, he did think about it; then he told my Sergeant I was trying to run his class. The Sergeant had me write a memo and run the Hill again. (Side note: The Department started, 2 years later, using circles, in baton training.) "Catch-22," again.

On my first day with a Field Training Officer (FTO) after getting out of the Academy, he told me "Forget everything you learned in the Academy; I will teach you how to be a real Street Cop". "Catch-22," again. I had had 2

Years' prior experience as a Police Officer, so I knew how to play the FTO- Rookie game: keep your mouth shut and do what you're told to do. Then, two weeks into my training, My FTO was driving and we were on the 3rd shift.

He started driving on dirt roads around Cordova Mountain. He drove from one dirt road to another for about 10 minutes, when he suddenly stopped and asked, "where are we, I just got shot and you have to get me some help." I looked at him and said: "I guess you're going to die; I'll bet you don't know how you got here, either." My FTO then asked me, "Do you have prior experience'? I told him, yep, two years, and I've played the "Where Are You?" game before. I was put on Solo duty a week later.

During my first week as Solo, I took a radio call, where on completion I could have written up a report in one of two ways. I asked Radio to have my Supervisor meet me at a location away from the scene. Upon my Supervisor's arrival, I explained the situation. His response was: "We pay you Big Bucks to make decisions. Do what you think is right; if it's wrong, I will let you know. If it's right, you will not hear a word from me." Then he drove off. I think, out of all the training I've gotten, his few words at that time had a major impact on me as to how to be a Police Officer. Use common sense; the rules are only guidelines. This marked the end of the "Catch-22" problems during my Rookie period, and in my 23 years,

I never got one Citizen Complaint, or Crime Report sent back for correction.

Kurt, after thinking back on my starting days, I was not a Rookie for very long. They had me working as an FTO two months after getting out of the Academy. In this day and age, it's unheard of.

(Niemann's note: I would imagine, or at least I would hope, that in most locations within the United States, training schedules for new Officers in Criminal Justice Agencies are no longer as primitive as those experienced by Curly and myself nearly forty years ago.)

## "CURLY" II – HOW WE LEARN

We had just rotated to the 3rd shift, and I had a Rookie assigned to me for training. The minute we left the station and were heading for our beat area, my Rookie fell sound asleep. I pulled over and woke him up. I then proceeded in trying to explain to him the hazard of falling asleep in a Police vehicle. In those days, you were lucky if you could hear the airwaves on the Police radio, after 2:00 A.M.    Come 2:00 A.M., guess who was sound asleep; I was driving, so it wasn't me. I had to wake him several more times before the end of the shift. The following shift it was the same story.

What's the old saying: "The 3rd time is the charm!" The third night, the same pattern was playing out. It was about 3:00 A.M., on a cold winter night, when my Police vehicle found its self along a canal bank, with the passenger door along the canal bank, which had approximately 3 feet of water running in it. All of a sudden my red lights came on, the siren started to blare and I started screaming, "Get that son-of-a-bitch!"

My young Rookie said: "Aw shit!" Then there was the splash, as he landed in the water! Strange thing, I never had to wake him up again.

*Chapter II*

# PROJECTS AND BARRIOS

## INTRODUCTION:

Early in the 1970's the Criminal Justice System decided to eradicate gangs by creating walking beats in projects and barrios and by developing groups of Police, Probation, and Parole Officers working closely together. The Los Angeles Sheriff's Department trained the primary officers in each unit assigned to deal with gangs.

Our streets were not as deadly as those in Los Angeles. But we did have our moments. This chapter will explore a few of our happy times.

Amazingly, we did not eradicate gangs.

# THE WALL

Long ago, those in political and economic power decided that whenever possible, economically disadvantaged folks should be provided low-or no-cost shelter, by the Government. Local, State and Federal Agencies coordinated the development of "Housing Projects;" usually multilevel multiple-family dwellings resembling large apartment complexes.

Law Enforcement Officers throughout the United States have, for the past several decades, seen these "Projects," as they are commonly called, to be synonymous with "gangs, drugs, and violence." While these labels certainly do not apply to all projects' residents---many are law-abiding persons, simply not financially capable of living anyplace else---crime in Projects is by no means rare.

"Barrio" is a term often used to define a Hispanic neighborhood within a city or town. This term, when applied, implies an identity separating "Our Dirt" from "Their Dirt." As applied by legitimate community activists and neighborhood helping agencies they help to create, the spirit behind the term "Barrio" is meant to exemplify all that is great in America. As applied by gangbangers living in the various "Barrios," it means Turf Wars is bound to occur.

In Metropolitan Cordova City, gang unrest became too evident to ignore by the early '70s. What I think made units of gang neighborhood specialists in Police, Sheriff's Departments, and Probation and Parole Departments inevitable, was the advent of drug-oriented turf wars; at the time, principally between the "Crips" and the "Bloods." These notorious gangs boasted members of predominantly "Afro-American" descent. By the time of the arrival of these gangs into Cordova City from Los Angeles, few Law Enforcement Officers in the United States had not at least heard of them.

These snakes first began to spread their venom in Cordova City at "The Wall."

"The Wall" had established its notoriety, simply due to the reason for its existence in the first place. When the City Fathers built the Projects known as "Pendleton Acres," two of the four multistory buildings comprising this Project were on either side of a major Cordova City thoroughfare. On both sides of the thoroughfare were the Projects' children's playgrounds. Excited children mindlessly running across the street were often struck and sometimes killed by passing cars. The solution: concrete walls, four feet high, were situated on either side of the Project, blocking traffic from passing through.

In a short period of time, for reasons known only to Pendleton Acres residents, every sort of Project resident miscreant began to assemble on the Eastside Wall. Members of the newly established gang unit have made it a practice over the last few decades to find a hiding spot in the area around the Wall, and photograph drug deals, stolen property sales, and fights. The Police Warrant section will be called in daily, to pick up one or another absconder, loitering at the Wall. I found it astounding that the thugs never learned. Fifteen years after I had left duty in the Projects forever, the Games at the Wall between bad guys and the Law Enforcement Agencies were still going strong.

The Crips first established their Cordova City cocaine dealing empire at the Wall. Like cancer, and at lightning speed, the Crips were soon all over the Metropolitan area. However, they did not operate without challenges: their chief competitor, the Bloods, arrived to fill the competition void.

Violence spread. A selected group of State and Local Law Enforcement Officers were dispatched to Los Angeles, California, for training in dealing with gangs and drugs. Cordova City's Police Officer Curly was one of those selected Officers to go to Los Angeles for Gang Training. Once trained, he and his colleagues reappeared in Cordova City, as Trainers for the rest of us.

Officers from the various Criminal Justice Agencies in our Metropolitan area were selected to deal firmly, quickly, and finally with "Inner City" gangs and drugs. Juvenile gangs, having rapidly become rampant---and very violent---in short order, a handful of Probation and Parole Officers were also selected to help eradicate the problem. We were not Line Police Officers and we were sorely in need of Gang training if we were going to be viable participants in this endeavor.

The Law Enforcement Officers recently Certified as "Gang Trainers" opened up a weeklong Academy for those of us who were to deal with this "Inner City problem." I was one of the Probation Officers chosen to be assigned to participate in these Specialized Units, I was to work in that part of Cordova City which was notorious for Hispanic Gangs, prostitution, and, how lucky for me, the Wall. We who were to be working in this area were therefore assigned to the Training Officer who would also be the Lead Officer for this geographic area.

It so transpired that the Lead Officer for my area was Curly. This is how my thirty-year professional relationship and everlasting friendship with Curly began.

The gangbangers we worked with actually saw us as "their" Cop and "their"

P.O. One of the benefits coming from this (besides not being shot at by them) was the information "our" gangbangers would regularly provide us regarding the illegal activities promulgated by other gangs in neighborhoods assigned to Officers other than ourselves. Of course, our 'bangers knew we were going to pass the information on to other Officers: that was the whole point---their rivals were going to be busted!

When I was working within the Inner City, I was usually transporting myself by way of my privately owned motorcycle. Besides being cheap and efficient to operate, there were other benefits to being on a motorcycle for me, such as having excellent visibility, so that I could see everything going on around me all the time. While on duty I usually wore a polo shirt, slacks, and shined lace-up boots. My Chief, whose Basic Agenda usually revolved around Image and Control, did on two occasions strongly advise that I stop wearing a black leather motorcycle jacket while on duty. Although it did severely traumatize my ego to do so, I ultimately did comply.

# BAT LADY

We would meet on occasion at a particular neighborhood crossroad, which was claimed by three different Hispanic gangs. On two of the corners of this intersection were concrete block walls, stuccoed, painted, and repainted regularly with "Placasos;" spray-painted testimonials to the most recent victories and defeats of those gangs claiming hegemony over the immediate turf.

Placasos are wonderful resources for those of us who need to know who is doing what, or doing whom. Usually very artfully painted in what I was told was called "Azteca" style, Hispanic gang-generated graffiti had a uniformity of application, making it possible for trained Law Enforcement Officers to decipher the latest neighborhood gang-related news as easily as though the painted walls were a printed tabloid. It, therefore, became a matter of routine to check out the assigned area's Placasos, the first thing every day.

These meetings served multiple purposes: making our presence known to the community, actual eye-to-eye contact for members of different agencies assigned to a geographic area, to work together toward a common goal.   They allowed us to get to know each other, and, on occasion, speak with each other frankly and outside the confines of our various Administrations' "party lines."

On one particular evening, we were aware, though being informed the day before on the local Placasos, that two of the three belligerent gangs in our area planned to amass their respective forces and settle this particular land dispute. Having an interest in the upcoming ritual, a few of those of us assigned to the area gathered and waited, Curly and myself included.

While the sunset sank and glowed a constantly deeper red in the West, the two gangs' heroes began to arrive and assemble. Most, if not all, were juveniles, and most of those were "Wannabes;" recruits in the gangs, needing to prove their value to their respective gang's leadership.

Imagine two groups of youth who have been ordered out by their respective leadership to battle over ownership of "the dirt." Neither group has been trained in unit tactics in urban terrain, or how to work together as a cohesive group. They have been given no Grand Plan of Operation. They all do have a highly deserved reputation for being reluctant to do battle individually; they want to fight only when they have a backup. No one knows when or how to begin the Rumble. They mill about mindlessly, across the street from each other, shouting epithets at each other, waving their weapons; mostly bats and chains. So far at least, no guns are visible.

Finally, there is nightfall; streetlights have come on and the verbal exchange between the antagonists intensifies. A small group from one of the gangs begins to cross the street menacingly toward the Enemy. The Enemy responds by retreating, en mass, probably not intentionally, into a neighbor lady's flower garden. That neighbor lady, an old and frail appearing gray-haired lady, flies out her front door, bat in hand, running toward and screaming at the gangsters who had trod upon her petunia bed. The retreating gangsters immediately intensify their retreat, scattering, as the screaming bat-wielding old lady runs down the sidewalk after them.

This War now being officially over, we who observed these gangbangers in action left the area for a local coffee house, eagerly looking forward to reading the description of this debacle on tomorrow morning Placasos.

# ON CITY RETIREMENT

Not all "gangbangers" in our assigned section of the inner city were "Hispanic," "Native American" or "African-American." I found myself dealing for half a year with two particularly vicious Anglo brothers. Their files came to me as Probationers (Strong-Armed Robbery). By the time a judge ordered them held for prosecution as Adults (they were 15 and 17 years old), they were well-known thugs, purse-snatchers, and car thieves. I rarely saw them dressed in anything other than filthy denims and in ragged t-shirts, which had possibly once been white. Their limited vocabulary was beyond vulgar. Whenever I spent time with them I worked very hard to keep in mind that most American youth, our future, actually are fine people.

Their father, when sober, was an electrician by trade. During the time his sons were on my Probation Caseload he went through a series of part-time jobs with T.V. repair shops. His main difficulty with employment was in leaving the bottle at home. In addition, he was paraplegic and therefore wheelchair-bound. Of greater interest to me was the young men's files reflected, in their Pre-Sentence

Investigation Reports, that their father's income came from two sources: Social Security, and retirement benefits from Cordova City.

At the time his sons were involved in the various court hearings which would conclude with an order they be remanded and jailed as Adults, the father was, for the time, clean and sober. During one Court Recess, we sat together at a County Court Building cafeteria table, nursing cups of black coffee. Running out of small talk, I said:

"Well, I hear you're on City Retirement?"

"That's right"

"What did you do for the City?" "Nothing."

"Well, I mean, what did you do...?" "I never worked for the city."

"But...?"

Then he told me how he came to obtain a pension from the city:

Ten years earlier, a Cordova City Police Officer was in high pursuit of a felon, Code Three, at night, in the area of a high-crime neighborhood.

Reports disclosed that the felony car and the pursuing Police car were at times exhibiting speeds exceeding ninety miles per hour. While at a high rate of speed, the Police Officer's car entered a dip in the road, bottomed out and the car's steering column broke. The police vehicle, now out of control, traveled approximately thirty yards off the street, onto the front yard of a private residence, and into the master bedroom of that residence. The vehicle struck the bed.

In the bed at the time were two people: a prostitute, and the man in the wheelchair with whom I was drinking coffee!

"So, that's how you ended up in a wheelchair?"

"Yep, I lost my legs, and I lost my wife when she found out I was with a hooker. But I sued the city and won."

And that's how the man came to have "City Retirement."

# DRUGS OF CHOICE

As is true in almost any other behavior in human life, "drugs of choice" will be largely a function of economics.

The image of a 16-year-old gangbanger snorting a line of coke at a party in a Barrio home is probably going to occur only in a Hollywood movie. Lines of coke are more likely to be snorted at parties where the participants can afford a $30,000 monthly drug habit. The combined monthly income of all the residents of an entire Barrio in Cordova City isn't likely to be $30,000.

Gangbangers who are committing burglaries, stealing cars for chopping and/or for transport to Mexico, and who are dealing in drugs, most often have to pass the money up to the Bigger Guys. Sixteen-year-old gangbangers do marijuana (when they can afford it), paint, gas, glue, and other kinds of low-cost substances, which are easy to acquire and abuse.

Early on during my career in the Inner City neighborhoods, gas sniffing was in vogue. Imagine all the formidable chemical substances from a gasoline-soaked rag that can find a way to the brain, to the blood, to the nervous system….

One afternoon in the mid-'70s, three young members of the Winfield Street Gang decided to get stoned under a gasoline-soaked wool blanket. They siphoned sufficient gasoline from someone's car to fill a bucket, and then they doused the blanket into the gas-filled bucket. Then they all crawled under the blanket so they could enjoy the benefits of the Petroleum Industry's product. During their resulting state of euphoria, one of the stoned "bangers" felt the need for a Marlboro. He lit up.

When the E.M.T.'s arrived (responding to a call regarding the resulting garage fire), two of the youths were pronounced dead at the scene. One youth spent several months in the County Hospital's burn unit and, barely, survived. Hopefully, he at least stopped sniffing gas.

Not far from Pendleton Acres there is a mortuary. Mortuaries typically contain embalming rooms within. Embalming rooms contain the chemical, Formaldehyde. For that reason, some gangbangers occasionally burglarized this mortuary. Marijuana laced with embalming fluid can provide, I am told, a truly brain-numbing kick.

Metal-flake spray paint was the all-time first-place winning drug of choice for juvenile and many adult gangbangers within my assigned area during my inner-city tenure. Metal-flake spray paint is made potent, I am told, by a particular chemical found only in the metal-flake varieties of spray paint.

This substance is generally inhaled by spraying the paint into a piece of fabric: a rag, a sock, or a towel, and then placing the paint-soaked fabric over the face.

So, how does one detect a paint sniffer? One's fingers and face covered with metal-flake paint often provide a clue. And it will not be unusual for the well-painted sniffer, nearly in a coma, to swear he has not been sniffing.

Curly had far greater opportunities than did I to see newly-reported dead people found inside a residence: generally, when a body is found, the Police were called first, and Curly was the Police. So it was that on a Particular Sunday, Curly and his patrol partner went to the home of nine-year-old Jamie Ramirez; to find Jamie lying in his bed, paint rag over his face, definitely deceased. His mother and his aunt were in hysterics: when you lose your child, a major part of your life will die as well.

Monday, one day after the death of Jamie Ramirez, I found Jamie's fourteen-year-old brother Pedro lying in a vacant lot, in a paint-induced stupor. I called Curly; together we loaded Pedro into a police vehicle for transport to Juvenile Detention. When he sobered up and a Detention Facility nurse cleaned the silver off his face, he swore he had not been sniffing paint.

On another occasion, Curly and I visited the home of 16-year-old gangbanger Jerry Velasco, a "Winfield Street Loco." Jerry loved to paint, so long as it was of the metal flake variety. I wised up at long last to Jerry's method of paint sniffing when one day I smelled the telltale odor of paint emanating from his ever-present can of Coke.

Mrs. Velasco opened the front door following our knock. When we approached the subject of Jerry's paint sniffing behavior, she launched into instant and loud denial. We asked her to allow us to walk into her backyard so we could show her what we could see by walking through the alley behind her house. Mrs. Velasco agreed and we walked into her backyard.

When we arrived at a structure in her back yard, which may have been, in better days, a chicken coop, we observed hundreds of empty metal flake spray paint cans. Still, Mrs. Velasco insisted that the paint was used only to "remodel Jerry's bedroom." She escorted us to Jerry's bedroom.

Yep, everything: ceiling, walls, bed, dresser, was painted silver. Well, said Mrs. Velasco, she hoped that this had taught us a lesson.

"PCP" is a chemical concoction initially developed, I have been told, as a veterinary anesthetic. Most often called "Angel Dust" on the street, it artificially produced the Mother of All Long-Lasting Adrenaline Rushes.

PCP-induced physical strength cannot be comprehended unless witnessed. One afternoon, "Curly" did have the opportunity to witness.

On an early afternoon, I was on the north side grounds area of the Pendleton Acres Projects, seated astride my trusty Honda 550 motorcycle, discussing recent Project events with a small group of local juveniles, when I heard, from a distance, a voice calls out:

"Hey, your white mother fucker!"

I looked around, and at length, I saw "Cat Daddy" Hanson. No surprise: he was so intoxicated and/or stoned it was a marvel that he could stand, much less shout.

The closer "Cat Daddy" approached, the more reluctant the youths around me became to remain nearby. Only two remained when Mr. Hanson stood on my left side, scowling down at me.

"What' cha doing' here, whitey?" His breath was activating my gag reflex. He smelled like a rotting corpse.

"Just catching' up on the Pendleton happenins', Cat Daddy. You O.K.?

"Fuck you, Neimann"

Before he finished bestowing this blessing upon me, I'd started my motorcycle. I dropped it into first gear, I said: "see ya, Cat Daddy," and I was gone.

Only minutes later, Curly and his partner, while walking on foot patrol through Pendleton Acres, noted "Cat Daddy" Hanson. While approaching "Cat Daddy" wisely, that is to say, very, very, cautiously, Curly used his 2- way hand radio to ask for more Officer backup.

Two Police cars appeared in rapid order. This presented "Cat Daddy" with Curly, Curly's partner, and four other uniformed Officers. Even at these odds, the Police were nearly overwhelmed: they were about to experience a very large person who hated cops, and who had been doing PCP and drinking beer all day.

"Cat Daddy" staggered toward the officers, attempting to run and shouting highly insulting terms toward them. The officers tackled him. Curly told me later that he immediately recalled his Aikido teacher's warning: "If you grab a Tiger by the tail, you may find that you cannot let go."

I am certain that this struggle would have met the demands of all but the most jaded of today's blood-and-guts moviegoers. Before they wedged "Cat Daddy" into a Police car's "cage," "Cat Daddy" had escaped the Officers, flailing at them with the one arm that still had a handcuff attached. One Police Officer was down with head injuries from being struck with the flying handcuff. All Officers were going to have to discard the shredded clothing they were wearing. Once again they tackled "Cat Daddy," with every once of strength they could muster, the burly, intoxicated creep was at last locked up in one of the cars.

The enraged "Cat Daddy" then tore the "cage," which is located behind the front seat of the car, loose from its mountings. He kicked the Police car door until the lock was shattered; the door flew open and only one door hinge was still partially held.

"Cat Daddy" was out loose once more, roaring his rage and still attempting to charge the Police Officers. His hands and one forearm were shredded.

Both ankles had been broken by kicking the Police car door off its' hinges. The defiant "Cat Daddy" still wanted to do battle.

Then, without warning, "Cat Daddy" dropped to the pavement, went into convulsions, and, at last, passed out. He was ambulanced to the County Hospital where, upon awakening, he entered into a lengthy, Court Ordered, taxpayer-financed, rehabilitation program. He would once again be in wonderful physical shape when, one year later, he commenced a somewhat lengthy, also Court Ordered, prison sentence.

Today, crack cocaine and crystal meth are often the drugs of choice of the gangbanger.

Volumes have been written about these evil substances and the lives that have been destroyed by their use. So why has no one learned? Why has the Government not done something?

In my opinion, the answers to those questions have been obvious all along. To respond to the first question, I refer the reader to the history of alcohol and alcoholism. It is clear that people who do not like or want the future they see in their lives will attempt to escape it. Some use alcohol, some use drugs, some use ropes, and guns, some use the police: anyone in law enforcement for a while will one day be exposed to "Suicide By Cop".

Well, what about the Government doing something?

Well. how many decades has the Government been fighting the Drug War? Fighting prostitution? Fighting pornography? Fighting polygamy in Arizona, Colorado, Utah, and a few other states? How about Prohibition?

Manufacturers and dealers of all evil and/or illegal products have known for millennia that so long as there is a demand, there are profits to be made, "Illegal" be damned. There yet remains, and so long as there are human beings in misery, there will continue to remain, a demand.

## CAT DADDY AND BATMAN

The aforementioned "Cat Daddy" Hanson was the oldest sibling in a family consisting of a single mother and eight children, all fathered by eight different lovers. "Skinny Winnie" Hanson and her brood lived in a Pendleton Acres Project apartment.

"Skinny Winnie" was very thin, very excitable, and, when flustered, she stuttered so badly it was nearly impossible to understand her. She was employed, part-time, with a janitorial company with contracts to clean downtown Cordova City offices. She was not necessarily quick to understand what was going on around her; consequently, her children enjoyed much freedom from parental control. Whenever I made contact with her, she was open and friendly. She always had a coffee pot going, and, as any Inner City Officer will tell you when food or drink is offered, protocol demands that you accept. She made excellent coffee.

"Cat Daddy" was a member of the Crips. He'd been in and out of Juvenile Court and detention facilities since he was ten, and now, following the encounter with Curly and his colleges as described earlier, at age twenty he was to find himself "inside the Walls." When he began that unfortunate afternoon by shouting "Hey You White Motherfucker," he had been only one day out of County jail.

I never did inquire into how "Cat Daddy" got his name. I had no desire to even guess.

"Batman" was "Skinny Winnie's" fourteen-year-old son at the time I joined the newly formed inner city unit. "Batman's" claim to fame was that he could burglarize a second or third story residence and, if necessary, exit through a window, loot in hand, run down the outside walls, and be running when his feet hit the ground. He had been detained no less than twice annually since his eleventh birthday, and he was on my Caseload.

My short involvement in "Batman's" life began with him in Detention, the day after Halloween. He had spent Halloween night strong-arming bags of candy from younger children. A parent accompanied one such group of children collecting candy. That parent, the father of one of the children being robbed, collared "Batman" and called the Police. When the Police arrived, "Batman" appeared to be somewhat the worse for wear.

In detention, "Batman" was one angry "Victim" of "That Mexican dude (the father of the victim child)". He swore he'd get even as soon as he goes out.

He did get out three weeks later, as a consequence of his public defender's successful appeal to the Court for release pending sentencing. Once out, "Batman" did take his revenge: he found the home of the man who'd had him arrested and conducted a "drive-by." He was rearrested and re-detained that same night. Within the week, "Batman" was a resident of the newly established "New Life" Juvenile Boys' Correction Facility.

Footnote: One of the many Games played, successfully, by Public Defenders to obtain release from detention for their clients is: "Holiday Spirit." Their basic approach is: what Juvenile Court Judge could be so heartless as to rip a child from the family nest during the Thanksgiving or Christmas season? Consequently, the population of many detention facilities is never so low as during the period between November 20th and January 2nd.

# STROLLIN'

At least as early as the late 1960s, mayhem and violence was occurring on occasion in the schools as well as on the streets. The attitudes and behaviors exhibited by the students who perpetrated the Columbine, Colorado, High School tragedy were not a new phenomenon: violence will occur anywhere that there are seriously troubled kids. (Ironically, the two Columbine juveniles had been "successfully" released from Juvenile Probation only a short time before they engaged in their shooting rampage). School officials will discover the nature of true administrative and emotional overload whenever offenders of any stripe decide to do their thing on a school campus. Police Officers are often assigned to patrol the perimeter of schools that are infested with gang activity. Perhaps it helps, perhaps not.

Offenses on school grounds will occur from time to time nevertheless.

A particular incident involving violence, which began on a Cordova City high school campus, sticks in my mind. Fortunately, there was no gunfire during this incident. The behavior of the news media during this incident did a lot toward galvanizing my cynicism toward that establishment. During lunch period at this high school, which is located in the Northwest section of the City a fight between rival gangs broke out in the students' parking lot. Curly, myself and about a dozen other Police officers were there; so, mysteriously enough, was the television media. As time went on, the fight migrated from the school parking lot to cross the street, onto another lot, where a strip mall was located.

At length, a member of the television crew broke out a loudspeaker and announced that the cameraman needed to change film canisters; could the combatants cease fighting until this film change was achieved? The fighting stopped. The entire crowd fell silent. Curly and I stared at each other, our jaws hanging down to our belts. Then, the television camera's film canister having been changed, the man with the loudspeaker announced the fight could resume.

At the request of the television crew, the fighting and the shouting and goading of the crowd did, in fact, resume. At last, many more Police Officers arrived at the scene and the majority of the crowd ultimately dispersed. A few gangbangers were arrested, and then we all moved on.

The next morning our team was back at the high school, hoping our presence might help discourage further outbursts. As students assembled onto school grounds, a police car with two officers inside pulled up to the light-controlled intersection on the northwest corner of the high school.

Their light was red at the time.

Strolling across the street, within the crosswalk, in front of the Police car were four African-American youths; they were in absolutely no hurry. The traffic light turned green for the officers. The youths stood in front of the car, smiling, appearing to be admiring the car's shiny chrome grille.

The light turned red. The youths strolled to the sides of the car and bade the officers "Good Day," then back to the front of the car to admire the bumper and the tires. The light turned green. The young men remained to check out the paint on the hood. The driver, a sergeant, was furious by now. He exited the car and loudly demanded that the youths leave. The light turned red. The youths, still grinning, bade the nice Officers a good day, and moved on, quickly disappearing into the crowd of students.

Grinning, Curly turned to face me and said, "You know, sometimes taking a little extra time to deal personally with attitudes like these kids just showed can make all the difference in the world. This kind of behavior reminds me of a little dance I had with our friend Ricky, the gangbanger with 8th Street. He used to just love to yell at cops, "Suck my dick; buy a lollypop and practice." He said this one time too many as he drove past my partner and me. We pulled his vehicle over and as Ricky started to say, "Suck…" he was pulled out of his vehicle through the driver's window. I laid him across the trunk, gently, of course, and very calmly, I advised him to call us Sir, Officer, or Detective. His response was "Yes Sir". I haven't had a problem with him ever since that meeting."

I had to admit, Ricky was always polite toward me.

# HIT GIRL

Sisters Sylvia Benitez, 15, and Celia Benitez, 13, were members of the "Fifth Street Locas," the "Ladies Auxiliary" of the Eighth Street Gang. Both girls were of a violent nature, aided, I believe, by a lot of paint sniffing.

Until her death at age 36, their mother was a prostitute and a heroin addict. Their father was an alcoholic; He hung onto life until he was 50; dying, I was told, incredibly painful death by hemorrhaging and convulsing. I did have the opportunity to briefly speak with Mr. Benitez a few days before his death. He was in a hospital bed, surrounded by extended family. Celia was with my supervisor and me. Celia was handcuffed, much to the dismay of the family.

Sylvia was on Probation, assigned to my partner's Caseload. She, and other 'Fifth Street Locas," was known for rolling drunks in the alleys of downtown Cordova City. On occasion, and this is how Sylvia found her way on Probation, she and her colleagues would pose as prostitutes, luring Johns into an alley. All the ladies together would then attack and rob the man or woman.

Celia was made of harder and more violent stuff than her older sister. She was as angry a juvenile as I'd seen, at least up to the time I met her. I have always believed that the basis for this anger was due to sexual activities her uncles had been engaging in with her for several years. When word of this behavior somehow got out, one of the uncles was convicted on a "Sex with A Minor" charge, and he did receive a stretch in prison as a result. In any event, Celia had a reputation for carrying a switchblade knife somewhere on her person at all times.

Celia was on my probation caseload, following a conviction for having nearly eviscerated a boy, an Eighth Street Loco, with her switchblade. The police report described a scene when several Fifth and Eighth Streeters were painting sniffing one evening, and during the event, the young man made sexual advances toward her; a very bad error of judgment on his part. She drew her knife and slashed him horribly. The Eighth Street gangbanger, now a victim survived. Celia was placed on Probation. She did serve one hundred twenty days in Detention as one term of Probation.

Celia's next notable exercise in violence occurred shortly after a "Winfield Street Loco" severely offended an "Eighth Street Loco" in some way or another. The offense could not stand unanswered. Celia was hired, for a case of metal flake spray paint, to address the issue with her trusty switchblade. During a class change at the high school, thirteen-year-old Celia Benitez walked up to the Winfielder, knife in hand, and stabbed him repeatedly in the abdomen. Celia fled immediately; however, other students had recognized her and she was given up to the police.

The boy survived. I interviewed him after his discharge from the County Hospital. His abdomen looked like a road map. Once again, Celia was convicted in Court on a charge of aggravated assault. This time, she was sent to the States Girls Juvenile Corrections Facility---which was located only three blocks from her home.

While awaiting the day for transport from our Detention Facility to the State's Girls' Juvenile Corrections Facility, Celia's father found his way to a County Hospital bed; His internal organs were at long last giving up their attempts to deal with the oceans of alcohol Mr. Benitez had consumed during his lifetime.

The Benitez family demanded that Celia be allowed to say goodbye to her father. The more we refused to release her for the visit the more vociferous they became. They called the Public Defender, the Judge, the local Latino activist, their County Board of Supervisors representative. At last, our Chief struck a deal with the Benitez family: Celia could go to the hospital, escorted by Niemen and Neimann's Supervisor. The family agreed to this arrangement.

My supervisor, a man in his late 50's at the time, had grown up in this neighborhood; he knew the Benitez family very well. He was certain, and he convinced me as well, that when we arrived with Celia, all the Benitez men would be present in the hospital room, and that they would try to prevent us from taking Celia back to Detention.

As it turned out, my Supervisor was right. However, Celia's right wrist was connected to my left wrist by handcuffs. As the level of Benitez family outrage rose, we made our departure. A few days later, Celia did make her appointment with the State Department of Juvenile Corrections.

# EVERYBODY HAS A STORY

Imagine a Latino family having the last name like "Grabitz". While working with gangs, I did encounter quite a few Latinos with German and Polish last names. According to my Latino Supervisor, an entire German colony had been established in Northern Mexico during the Nineteenth Century. These people had been contracted by the Mexican Government as building and road construction workers. During their free time, the workers met and liked Mexican ladies. Many workers married and remained in Mexico, where they raised families and continued to prosper.

The "Godfather" of the "Los Latinos Locos" gang was Benny Grabitz. Benny was in his late 50's when I became involved with his immediate family. Benny was a chain-smoker. He had what his wife told me was a terminal case of emphysema, yet I rarely saw him without a cigarette. He always had a large oxygen tank on wheels next to him. He would remove the oxygen tubes from his nose, take a puff from his cigarette, and then bring the tubes back to his nose. He had the physical movements down pat. One would expect such precision from the Godfather of a gang.

Mrs. Grabitz was a trim, serious lady, also in her 50's. She was employed full-time as a Captain with a Security Company. I never saw her out of her uniform. Even when she was not physically present in the Grabitz home, I saw her in uniform: The three walls of the living room were replete with numerous eight-by-ten sized photographs of Mrs. Captain Grabitz in her uniform. She never spoke with me about her job; She would merely stand in my presence, scowling, and making certain that I saw the "tracks" on her collar.

Steve Grabitz was on my Probation Caseload. He was a part of the membership of the section of the "Los Latinos Locos" that stole cars, ran them through a "chop shop," and sold the parts. He was as sneaky as was his mother prim and proper in her uniform. It seemed that "everybody knew" what he was doing: the placasos often proclaimed his derring-do, but it seemed that building a prosecutable case against him was forever going to be difficult indeed.

Steve's sixteen-year-old girlfriend lived with the Grabitz family for nearly two years. She was still there when I was assigned to Steve's case, but she left the Grabitz home a few months later to live with her new, lesbian, lover, the notorious strong-arm robber, and paint sniffer Brenda Martinez. Brenda wouldn't allow me to speak with Steve's erstwhile girlfriend.

Brenda told me: "Steve's too rough with her. I know how to treat her right".

One fine evening, Steve and his older brother, Tony, got into a hassle with the Police during an attempt to commit an armed robbery of a convenience market. Tony shot and killed one of the Officers. Tony, always a very violent gang "Veterano," went to prison, hopefully forever. Steve was remanded for Court processing as an Adult. He was convicted, and he received a seven-year sentence.

Mr. And Mrs. Grabitz always steadfastly insisted that they "Knew nothing about any gangs." They also steadfastly proclaimed to the end that their sons were "Railroaded" by the Cordova City Cops.

# THE INNOCENTS

While I was dealing with the Grabitz Family, I came to realize that the Rascon's, a family residing a block away from the Godfather, were among the chief movers of residential burglary goods brought in by members of "Los Latinos Locos." I was, one day, severely brought to task in Court and, later, at my office, by a Public Defender who took umbrage at the thought of a Rascon being involved with crime (Are you surprised?).

At the arraignment hearing of young Vincente Rascon, who was one of the "Los Latinos Locos" gangbangers, on a burglary charge, I asked the Court to continue to detain the young man on the basis of a long string of burglary allegations, and on my belief that he was a major player in the trafficking of stolen residential property with the rest of the Rascon Family. The Judge ordered Vincente to be continued detained.

My Behavior in court seriously annoyed Vincente's Public Defender, one Juliet Blake, B.A., J.D., Ph.D. (Psychology,) AKA "Sweet Julie" by her many detractors. Those of us who tended to dislike her would call her Sweet Julie" only out of her earshot, of course. "Sweet Julie" was nothing if not arrogant, abrasive, and tenacious. She took it upon herself to conduct a records check on Mr. And Mrs. Rascon (no record), contact them, advise them of my scurrilous comments about them in Court; and then escort them physically to my office for a confrontation with me, and to demand an apology.

Prior to the arrival of the Armada of Sweet Julie and Mr. And Mrs. Rascon, I called my best Police contact, "Curly," of course. I told him about Sweet Julie "going ballistic" during and after Court, and that I planned on some fallout coming in soon. Curly told me: "don't sweat the petty stuff, we're building paper on those people."

Having Curly's assurance in hand, I greeted Sweet Julie and the Rascon's with an open office door and a friendly greeting. Sweet Julie stood out in the hallway, shouting my incompetence to the world in her usual outrageous fashion. I most humbly apologized to the Rascon's. Then, they all went away. Sweet Julie's client, the Los Latinos gangbanger, remained, of course, in Detention.

Two weeks later, the Cordova City Police, warrants in hand, raided the Rascon residence, garage, and shed. They left with several vans loaded with stolen residential property.    They also left with Mr. And Mrs. Rascon, handcuffed of course.

Because I believed a well-informed Attorney can best serve her clients, I made certain that a copy of the local newspaper's article describing the Rascon home raid found its way on Sweet Julie's desk.

## LOS MOJADOS

By far, the largest and most violent Latino gang to be established in Cordova City area was "Los Majados (pronounced, "Moe-hah-doez"). The name translates, loosely, as "The Wetbacks."

Conventional Wisdom has eternally had it that "Wetback" is an epithet, universally regarded as the most grievous insult one can direct toward a person of Hispanic descent. Yet, when "Los Mojados" appeared on the gangbanger scene, it was obvious that this gang had deliberately chosen the name as an "in-your-face" primarily to the "Chicanos" population; that is, those Latinos who are native to North America but have Mexican ancestry. "Los Mojados" gangbangers take pride in the fact that they are illegal aliens. To be more Politically Correct, I should say they are "Undocumented Immigrants."

Being an Illegal Alien has some very real advantages when apprehended by police. After a moderate stay in one detention facility, the Illegals are usually deported. After deportation, they often return as quickly as a Yo-yo, with new false identity papers and plenty of safe havens to run to. The Federal and Local Authorities, during my career, were constantly at odds with each other as to policies and procedures for coping with arrested Illegals, the juveniles in particular. Yes, there were agreements between Government agencies, but from my position, I always was of the opinion that in any given circumstance, whenever the Feds could walk away from responsibility for their screwups and lay it all on the Locals, they would do so.

A "Mojado" named Pedro Garros was one of the first to bring to my attention the reality that not all gangbangers were 24-hour-per-day violent killers and rapists. Seventeen-year-old Pedro resided with his extended family in a small apartment complex on the Southern edge of "Los Mojados" dirt. The extended family occupied the entire apartment complex. Pedro lived in one of the apartments with his mother, a younger sister, and two younger brothers. His nineteen-year-old girlfriend and his infant son lived in another apartment within the complex.

Pedro was on probation for auto theft. At the time he was on my Caseload for two years with no further arrests, I came to believe that I needed to devote more energy to cleaning out my overly-stocked file cabinet full of very active cases; let's release Pedro from probation.

Pedro held two jobs, both in local fast-food eateries. His earnings supported himself, his mother, his siblings, his girlfriend, and his son. He'd told me very early on in our relationship that he'd joined "Los Mojados," the gang ruling the turf on which he resided, partially to stay alive, and partially to ensure his family's safety. At least, so he told me…

I wrote a "Report and Review" brief, describing Pedro's background, arrest and conviction, and his progress while on Probation. The Presiding Judge returned my brief, through interoffice mail. On it, written across the first page, in large, red letters, was the word: "Denied!"

Somewhat taken aback, I discussed Pedro's case with my Supervisor, Pedro's public defender, and also with Pedro's prosecutor. None could understand why the denial. I approached the Presiding Judge. He said:

"I want him prosecuted." "But, Your Honor, why?"

The Presiding Judge scowled at me and said:

" You stand right there and read your Report!" I did so. The Presiding Judge said, "well?" "Judge, I can't see…"

His Honor grabbed the file from my hands, His face turning red; he pounded on the face of my Report. "This offender is living in Open And Notorious Cohabitation!" Yelled The Presiding Judge. He then tossed the Report at me, told me to file a Complaint of Probation Violation complaint with the prosecutor's office, and then told me to get the hell out of his sight.

"Open And Notorious Cohabitation." Seventeen-year-old Pedro Garros was residing in one apartment; his nineteen-year-old girlfriend and his infant son were residing living in yet another apartment. On the Streets, various City, County and State Law Enforcement Agencies were working on gangbangers who were infesting the City with drugs, violence, and property felonies; and the Presiding Judge saw Pedro being prosecuted because Pedro was not married, a clear violation of the law, as a major issue.

The Lord knows I would never wish to be in Contempt of Court; I immediately took the file to the prosecutor who had handled Pedro's case. The prosecuting attorney heard me out. He said: "Bullshit."

Of course, Pedro was not prosecuted. Later, Pedro enjoyed his eighteenth birthday and was therefore released from Probation and out of the jurisdiction of the Juvenile Justice System.

## MS. PAC-MAN

Street Cops and Street Caseworkers should never wear suits, sports coats, and ties when rubbing shoulders with the residents of Projects. (Those loud gasps of horror you are now hearing are emanating from all Agency Chiefs and Directors who want all Caseworkers to "Dress Professionally;" basically, wear suits.) In the Inner City, this is a Bad Idea. Many economically disadvantaged folks, whose entire wardrobe may have cost less than your tie, will resent you for representing yourself, at least in their perception, as being superior to them. While they may find your out-of-place attire to be somewhat humorous, they may also decide that you are possibly a bill collector or a car repossessor. Such people, when encountered in the Projects, have been known to end up being beaten and/or shot.

If you work in economically disadvantaged neighborhoods, wear casual clothing and be yourself. Do not put on airs; do not lead with your ego. The people you contact will want to know: what do you intend to do in their neighborhood? Will you be a positive element in their community, or are you a threat to everyone; ordinary citizens, perpetrators, and victims alike? Once you have been identified, at least by your job within a given agency, you will discover that many of the people you are contacting know your job better than you do. And they can detect "Phony" as soon as "Phony" arrives in the neighborhood.

If you follow these simple guidelines, whether Cop, P.O., or Social Worker, you will discover you will likely be at least treated humanely, and probably with respect. You never know, you may someday find yourself in need of assistance from the people you have been sworn to serve.

On a particular October morning, because I was scheduled to spend the entire day in Court, I "dressed up" as formally I was ever willing to do so, in civilian clothing: slacks, single-colored shirt, tie, sports coat. I can assure you that to walk into His Honor's Courtroom without wearing a coat and tie would incur His Honor's Wrath, which few were ever willing to have to face. Dressed for Court, I mounted my brand new V-twin motorcycle and braved morning rush hour traffic all twenty-four miles to the Court Building.

By five p.m. that day, I was exhausted. Lots of things can drain an Officer Of The Court: waiting two hours for a ten-minute hearing to begin (commonplace), listening to Public Defenders and defense witnesses blame everybody and everything but the Accused of the crime; wondering when the Chief Prosecutor will fire his more incompetent attorneys rather than simply assigning them to your Cases, listening to lengthy testimonials from Reverends and relatives regarding how the defendant "Found Jesus" while in jail and so must be given yet another "Pass"…

As I readied myself to exit the Superior Court Building that afternoon, His Honor's Bailiff approached me: the Judge wanted me to inform a family residing in my assigned area that a Warrant For Nonappearance had been issued for their son, who was a "Crip." Not being one to turn down the wishes of the Presiding Judge, I accepted a copy of the Warrant and agreed to comply.

After Court was over, I mounted my brand new, week-old motorcycle and rode off into Crip territory, sport coat and tie and all. I arrived at the residence just before sunset. I parked in a vacant dirt lot next to the home and was greeted by the subject Crip, his girlfriend, his four-year-old little brother, and his parents. Of course, they knew me.

"Watchoo want whitey?" asked my recently – Warranted Crip. "I was told you didn't show up for court today."

"Huh? I dint have no Court today."

"Well, the Judge thought that you did, and since you weren't there, he issued a Warrant for you."

"Bullshit."

"I've got it right here, but the Judge said I didn't have to bring you in (right---on the back of my motorcycle?), I should just give this to you and you can go see him tomorrow morning."

I handed the copy of the warrant to him. "Okay."

That issue having been resolved, I mounted my motorcycle and – the ignition key was missing!

I looked at the ignition socket. I looked around on the ground. Nothing. I dismounted and searched my pockets. Nothing.

"' Zup, Niemann?"

"Man, my bike key is missing."

"Shit man, it's getting dark, let's look for it."

It's true: the entire family, sans the four-year-old, all got on their hands and knees, looking for my missing motorcycle key. However, no luck.

At last, the four-year-old child owned up to having removed the key and having fun with it. He had no idea where he'd laid it down.

How wonderful. My spare key was at home, twenty-six miles away. I could not just abandon my brand new motorcycle in Crip territory and call a cab. I needed to call home and have the spare key brought to me.

The Crip's family had no telephone. The nearest telephone – a pay telephone – would be at "Sandy's Corner", a notorious liquor store and Black gangbanger meeting center, located on the Northeast corner of a major intersection in the immediate area.

So, sports coat, tie, and all, I put my motorcycle's transmission into neutral and walked it through the dark, unlit neighborhood, and, finally, to Sandy's Corner.

Lots of interesting folks were always hanging out at Sandy's Corner, some perhaps sober, but mostly not. Once again, I parked my motorcycle in front of Sandy's Liquor

Store and walked up to the pay telephone. I was the only Anglo present, sportscoat, tie and all.

I called home. No answer. I called my next-door neighbor, Don Moran. Don and his wife had a key to our home: when we were on vacation, they watched our home, and vice versa.

Don answered my call. I told him of my dilemma and where my other motorcycle key was. Don laughed, thought the whole thing was a real knee-slapper, and told me he'd be at Sandy's Corner in an hour. I had to give Don detailed travel instructions: He'd never before needed to drive into this particular part of Cordova City.

So, there I was, all dressed up, and in the wrong place to be. I sat on my bike, constantly being watched by curious eyes, and not a familiar, or friendly-appearing face in sight. Not a Cop in the area. None of my Hispanic gangbangers, either: they dared not show in this area at night. I sat. I sat some more.

A woman's voice behind me said: "what are you doing here, Niemann?"

I turned around. At last, a friendly face: a hooker I was acquainted with! Okay, this hooker was also the mother of one of my Probationers. She smiled and said again: "what are you doing here Niemann?

I told her my sad story, and that I guessed my neighbor Don would be here within the next half hour. She said: "C'mon Niemann, let's play some Ms. Pac-Man. Your bike is okay there by the door."

So it came to be that my next-door neighbor drove into the parking lot of Sandy's Corner, walked into Sandy's

Liquor Store, and found me playing Ms. Pac-Man with a hooker. He never let me forget about it, either. My other neighbors also enjoyed the story.

## CUFFING THE COP

The day after I learned how to play Ms. Pac-Man, I rushed to Curly's favorite hideout (no, not a donut shop), because I wanted to be the first of what I knew from experience would be several dozen reports of "Niemann and the hooker at Sandy's Corner". Of course, he'd already heard. I knew that this would be one of those events Curly would never let me forget.

Curly waved a greeting, with a bandaged right hand and wrist. I immediately launched into a lecture on how masturbation could render one blind and also injure one's wrist. However, the actual story around Curly's wrist was far more interesting.

While I was playing Ms. Pac-Man, Curly and a dozen other officers were attempting to quell a fight between two rival pimps on Cordova City's infamous center of prostitution, California Street. Pimps are typically not the kind of people one would wish to aggravate; they can be violent. I once had occasion to observe a pimp settle a dispute by the use of razor blades held between his fingers.

However, quell the pimps they did: more than a dozen officers, some in uniform, some in civilian attire, writhing about on the ground in a "Doggie Pile," arms flailing and handcuffs flashing....

Curly told me he remembered shouting "Hey, Goddammit, that's MY wrist!" No one heard; Curly felt the cuffs clampdown, very tightly.

When all was over, Curly's right hand was red and blue; his wrist was badly bruised and had shed some blood. Finally, another Officer did remove the cuffs and an EMT dressed his wrist. Curly asked around for the owner of the errant set of handcuffs; no one seemed willing to admit to being missing a set. Back at the Police Substation, Curly presented the handcuffs to the Shift Commander. I am certain the Commander ultimately located the owner of the cuffs. I am certain that the owner of the cuffs was grateful as well.

## SHALLAH

Jackie Ford was a hooker. Jackie was a cross-dresser; his street name was "Shallah."

Typically, on California Street, female prostitutes occupied the South side and the male prostitutes, including the "Trannys," occupied the North side. Toward this section of the City, most female prostitutes were Black, residing in the nearby Projects; further East, the prostitutes were more
commonly runaway teenage girls from other locations, or very worn out, usually middle-aged, white women, from the nearby trailer parks. Male prostitutes were most often teenaged boys. Some male prostitutes were young adults, true "Trannys," undergoing various stages of hormonal,

silicone, and/or other surgical and chemical therapies. "Trannys" were sometimes blatantly obvious, but could also be stunning as a "woman." My own rule of thumb concerning prostitutes on both sides of the street was "if she's clean and somewhat attractive, she's a Tranny or she's a Vice Cop." This was, of course, not always true: some Vice Cops were ugly.

Jackie ("Shallah") dressed as a "woman" when "working." A sixteen-year-old, two-hundred-sixty pound, African-American youth from the nearby "Italian Gardens" projects, his "station" was at the bus stop located at the intersection of Twentieth and California Streets.

Shallah's wardrobe included some of the most stylish attire one could hope to shoplift at the best shops in one of Cordova City's nearby upper-level economic suburbs. I recall sitting one morning in a Section Meeting when one of my colleagues declared: "Neimann, those hookers in your area are really blatant. Yesterday, I saw one of the Black hookers on Twentieth and California walking around totally topless!"

Curly and I looked at each other and grinned. Curly said to me "are you gonna tell him or am I?" I said to our colleague: "Sam, that hooker was a male. His street name is Shallah. He has big boobs because he weighs two hundred sixty pounds. You gonna bust a guy for walking around shirtless?"

Sam's face and neck turned red. He was quiet for the rest of the meeting. The only way to describe "Shallah's" life history is: tragic. He had been in and out of foster homes from age four to twelve; he constantly ran away from those homes and always returned to his parent's Projects apartment. At length, Child Protective Services would do no more; then, Jackie found himself on probation (shoplifting). He wore out several Probation Officers (NO! NO! NO! He wore them out AS CASEWORKERS!) before his Probation File found its way to my desk.

Jackie's mother was a four hundred pound practicing Bisexual. I had actual contact with her on two occasions: once in her apartment, an "honor" not usually bestowed upon Law Enforcement Officers, and once in Jail. Her arrest and booking at that time occurred when she was observed in a department store to take a boxed television set from a shelf and place it on the floor. This lady always wore clothing best described as a "loose and comfortable," e.g., a "Muumuu." After having placed the thirteen-inch television set on the aisle floor, store security personnel observed her squat down over it, clasp it between her ample thighs and then rise and, waddling, attempt to depart the store!

Jackie's father, also a Bisexual, ran off with his "Gay" lover and disappeared well before I was assigned to Jackie's Case.

I always found it curious that many of the young male prostitutes I knew claimed to be regularly entertaining downtown Cordova City's business "Elite," as their afternoon clientele. I find it difficult to understand how these highly educated, socially and economically highly-placed "Suits" could elect to engage in such outrageously stupid and destructive, not to mention Criminal, behavior, thereby endangering themselves and their families. I do recall a number of cases verifying the claims of the young male hookers. It was only a few years before this book was written that a well-known male movie star was arrested, in my old former Inner City area, with one of these fellows.

How dangerous can it be? Well, for example, the Latino "Eighth Street Locos" was famous for posing as male prostitutes, then robbing and, Occasionally, killing their hapless victims. My first experience in such an event involved the "Eighth Street" killing of a Cordova City clergyman.

That fellow, in fact, had enjoyed a highly publicized reputation as a Youth Leader at his church. You never know...

And, of course, the prostitutes themselves could be badly beaten, and, sometimes, killed, as well.

Most of my contacts with Jackie were at my local "Community Office, during times when he was attired in regular, "off duty," clothes. He was usually friendly and had a supercharged sense of humor. As can be the case with prostitutes, Jackie was a terrific source of street information for me.

One of my contacts with Jackie will never be forgotten, if for no other reason than Curly will not allow me to forget:

In its' day, the Kawasaki 650 motorcycle was the fastest and most powerful motorcycle in its class. For several years I rode this four-cylinder two-wheeled rocket in and out of downtown Cordova City traffic, loving every moment. One fine afternoon, my "Kaw" and I were cruising Eastbound on California Street, and there on the "women's" side of the street stood Jackie. I stopped to exchange greetings. To my surprise, Jackie was wearing makeup, from the neck up. Seeing my surprise at the carefully made-up face and bright red hair, he said:

"Don't worry Niemann, I'm not working." "Okay."

"I'm gonna get all this shit off my face as soon as I get to my room." "Okay."

"Hey, you can help me, if you'll give me a ride. It's just a few blocks further down . . ."

"Okay. Hop On."

At this point, my brain told me "idiot! You're gonna regret this!" But Jackie/Shallah was already seated on the back seat of my bike.

The added two-hundred-sixty pound weight on the back of my mighty Kawasaki 650z brought its' front wheel off the pavement. As I added throttle, I leaned forward, bringing the front wheel at least slightly back down onto the road. Meanwhile, Jackie/Shallah held on tightly to my waist. Before we covered one hundred yards of California Street, Jackie/Shallah shouted into my left ear: "Hey Niemann, looky there." "There," cruising alongside us, situated in the left lane, was a car full of my unit colleagues.

They were all grinning from ear to ear.

And of course, Curly knew all about it before my bike's engine had cooled down.

# THAT DIDN'T HURT!

Jose was not necessarily the quickest of thinkers amongst his paint sniffing and car-stealing companions in the Winfield Street gang. When he was younger, Jose was one of Curly's "pet projects," a kid with some promise, but he was losing that promise, due to paint sniffing. As time went by, we could observe the kid's drop in I.Q. through brain-killing paint fumes. You can't adopt and save them all.

Jose was not on my caseload, but I ran across him a lot. Despite all other aspects of his life, he did have an engaging sense of humor. I hope that this quality helps him throughout what I suspect will always be a tough life. For example:

One evening, Jose and two other "Locos" obtained a car from Sylvia Benitez (you've read of her earlier), AKA, "The Queen Of Column Crackers." As they toured Downtown Cordova City (it's called "joyriding")' they came to discover that they were being followed not by one, but by two, Cordova City Police cars, their overhead "Visibar" lights announcing a need for the Winfield Street Locos to pull over, stop, and exit the stolen car, arms extended and hands on the hood.... The driver of the stolen car elected instead to draw out his handgun, extend it out the driver's side window, and open fire back at the following Officers.

When I spoke with Jose of this incident, he was residing in detention at the time, awaiting sentencing on Conspiracy and other felony charges. He told me that when the Felony Pursuit began, he was in the front passenger seat of the stolen car. He said that when the Officers' lights came on, the driver of the stolen car panicked; he pulled out his handgun and commenced to fire the gun back, in the direction of the Officers. Jose told me he wrestled the handgun from the driver and, as he tossed the gun out the window, the driver lost control of the stolen car and crashed. Jose was thrown out of the car.

As Jose was lying on the pavement, the lead police car rolled over him. Fortunately, the Police car's tires did not touch him.

All three cars, the crashed stolen car and the two cars driven by the Police, came to a stop. Miraculously, Jose was battered but not seriously injured. Jose then tried to get up and get off the street. As Jose explained it to me, he could feel what he believed was blood on his forehead. He reached into his pocket to draw out his bandana to wipe his face. Before his hand left his pocket, an Officer from Police car number two shot him, twice, in the chest.

Following a week in County Hospital, Jose was now in Detention. He said to me: "But it's ok – it didn't hurt."

# TATTOOED BUT NOT SCREWED

Two "Eighth Street Locos" stand out in my mind as examples of young men who were gangbangers, then left the barrio, became successful businessmen, then returned to the barrio – as volunteers in a neighborhood youth program.

David and Jerry (Geraldo) Jackson were the issue of a Mexican National mother and an Anglo father. When David was fourteen and Jerry twelve, their father found a younger lady to his liking in a topless bar, sold his small plumbing business, bought a Mercedes Sports car, and spirited himself and his formerly topless honey off, to parts unknown.

David and Jerry's mother was employed in the County Hospital laundry until arthritis crippled her hands and did serious damage to her spine. From that time on, she collected "Disability" and attended herself to her sons.

Don't even ask about her receiving "Child Support."

As David and Jerry's testosterone levels increased through adolescence, the lure of "gangbanging" became sufficiently attractive to lure them out of school and onto the streets. David found his way on my Probation Caseload after a series of car thefts. Jerry, fourteen when his Probation File was assigned to me, was a tall, skinny, angry, and defiant gangbanger and a constant fighter. He found his way into my file cabinet with a strong-arm robbery conviction.

David was a quiet youth. He decided his first conviction would be his last, and it was. He was visibly crushed by his mother's anguish over her sons being watched by the Badge. He disappeared from the gangbanging scene, got a job with a fast-food establishment studied for a High School G.E.D., then attended college classes.

That fast-food job, however, was not David's first job. He began his employment history as a movie projectionist. Yes, his mother proudly called one day to tell me, her

David had found a job as a projectionist at a movie theater. When I asked, she told me she didn't know the name of the theater, but she did know the location.

I grinned when she told me of the location. I was positive I knew the name of the theater, but I decided to take my motorcycle up there to find out for certain. Yes, it was a porno movie theater! I walked in the front door and sure enough, sixteen-year-old David Jackson was operating the movie projector. He looked back at me, smiled, and said: "Wait a minute." He called to the manager and said: "This is my P.O.; I hafta quit." He drew his paycheck and walked out of the theater with me.

Jerry Jackson was of the same mother, but not of the same disposition. The second time I saw him he had one arm in a sling, swollen eyes, and a broken nose. He had lost a fight with a gangbanger from a rival gang. He'd discovered that his bare hands could not match the power of a bat.

Jerry was a very talented artist. As such, he amassed large sums with his tattooing equipment. Regardless of gang affiliation, Jerry figured everybody's money was good. His skin-art work spread quickly over Cordova City's gang areas. His work spread all over his own body as well. Only his hands, neck, and face remained untouched by the time Jerry retired his needles.

Eventually tiring of losing far more fights than he won, Jerry decided to pay heed to his brother's advice and his mother's pleas; he got a job with a janitorial outfit. It was ideal for Jerry: he could be out all night and sleep all day.

As far as I knew, if David and Jerry had been engaged in drug or other substance abuse, they must have quit at an early stage. As time went on David obtained his High School G.E. D and an Associate's Degree from the County Junior College System and a B.S in Business from one of the local Universities. David shrewdly saw a future in the computer industry. He made a valuable contact in California, moved to that State, and immediately began to draw a wage far overshadowing mine.

Jerry Jackson rose to a management position in his Janitorial Company. He then bought the company. Then he bought another Janitorial Company and merged the two. Finally, Jerry sold his Janitorial Company and bought a Real Estate Franchise. In his first year in Real Estate, his income was greater than any three years of mine.

Summers are hard on Jerry; he always has to wear long sleeves and a tie to hide his tattoos.

And, yes, the brothers did buy their mother a house in a beautiful upscale suburban neighborhood. They do also provide her with the pension she so totally deserves.

# CURLY III

We had this female Police Officer who thought her shit didn't stink. She truly thought she was the gods' gift to Man. She was selected by the Vice Division to act as a hooker on California Street. We were assigned to be the Hit Car for the Johns that offered her a deal.

The female officer wore a body mike and we had videotape running inside an RV, with a T.V. monitor. It was nighttime. The first John in a vehicle pulled up beside her. The conversation went as follows:

John: "What are you doing?" Officer: "Working."

John: "What are you working at?"

Officer: "What would you want me to be working at?"

John: "How about in a Zoo; you're so fucking ugly, I wouldn't even throw peanuts at you!"

At this point, the john drove off. The raving Doll Officer reached into her bra, and pulling out the body-mike, started screaming into it:

"Stop that son-of bitch, he is under arrest, isn't this fucking mike working; Arrest him!"

The female officer working with her got a $25 offer for a blowjob, just two minutes after replacing God's Gift to Man.

# CURLY IV

Starr was one of our regular hookers working California Street. My partner and I were on our way one day to lunch when we observed Starr getting into a brand new white vehicle occupied by an old white guy. We followed the vehicle one block South to the hooker's favorite parking lot. My partner went to the driver's side of the vehicle and I opened the passenger door and told Starr to get her ass out of the vehicle. I directed her back to our Police vehicle. At that point, I asked Starr if she had any idea who she got in the car with. She said, "No! He was only giving me a ride".

I said, "Starr, that was the Mad Turk!" She asked, "Who is the Mad Turk?" I related that he is well known for having a camel hair whip in the trunk of his vehicle and that he loves to beat the ladies with it and that I didn't want to see her get her ass whipped by him. She thanked me and tried to hug me. I told her to let the other ladies know about him. She went back to California Street and started telling all the hookers about the Mad Turk. We then told the old man that Starr had a 25 Auto, and was going to rob him. I don't think the old man, AKA "The Mad Turk," will ever be able to buy a piece of ass in Cordova City!

## CURLY V

We received a radio call to give medical aid (this was before Fire Department Paramedics). Upon arrival, a crying woman told me her husband was on the bedroom floor and was not breathing.

I walked back to the bedroom and observed a heavy-set Mexican male, approximately 35 years old, laying face up on the floor. I observed a hypodermic needle in his right arm. Both arms were loaded with track marks. Kneeling beside him was another male, approximately the same age.

The man told me his friend was not breathing and that he wanted me to help him perform CPR.

I checked the man for a pulse; he did not have one. He was also cold to the touch. By this time several other family members arrived and they were all screaming, "Help him!" So, being the lifesaver that I am, as the friend started mouth to mouth and I did heart compressions. The friend did not have the dead guy's head tilted back far enough; the dead guy up-chucked into the friend's mouth. The friend spits out the vomit, wiped the dead guy's mouth off, and continued the mouth-to-mouth. The dead guy up-chucked again into the friend's mouth. At this point, the friend said, "Officer, take over, I'm going to get to get sick," and left the bedroom.

The family members were still screaming, "Help him! I told them they had to leave the bedroom, so I could work. They all left; I shut the door, walked over to the dead guy, and pronounced him dead.

As a side note, the heroin that the dead guy had injected was 90% pure. He must have pissed off someone.

*Chapter III*

# "INKYS:" THOSE STATUS OFFENDERS"

## INTRODUCTION:

Disobedience, runaway, violence between parents and kids: what's wrong with those damned kids and families, anyway? This chapter contains a lot of heartburn and precious little antacid. I discovered that there are two kinds of parents: those who said their children never gave them serious problems, and those who were truthful.

# WHAT IS AN "INKY?"

It has always been my opinion that the Legal System in general, and the Criminal Justice System in particular, sees Juvenile Issues as a necessary, but usually distasteful, field to deal with. Ordinary citizens' attitudes toward Juvenile issues, i.e., delinquents, foster kids, runaway kids, will vary, usually according to ones' own life experiences and education, but generally, the Conventional Wisdom is: "It's the parents' fault!"

Police see juvenile offenders as a great source of frustration, "Because no one does anything about them anyway," and because "They're out of jail before the ink is dry on my report!

I suspect that most Trial Court Judges actively avoid taking the Juvenile Bench. I say this because, in my experience, Juvenile Court Judges are the hardest and longest working souls in the legal field. They typically are in their Chambers (office) before anyone else's car is in the Court parking lot. They are also the last to leave, and usually with a stack of Court Files going home with them. It is my observation that the majority of Trial Court Judges in the other divisions, E.G., Criminal, Probate, Divorce, etc., do not bear nearly the burden carried by Juvenile Court Judges.

I believe Prosecuting Attorneys and Public Defenders assigned to the Juvenile Division often accept their posts reluctantly and see this assignment as an administrative punishment. And, sadly, sometimes it is.

I saw few private attorneys take on Juvenile issues; generally, the ones who did were essentially volunteers who offered their services to the Presiding Juvenile Judge. The Judge would assign them to cases when issues arose around legal conflicts of interest, and also as "Guardians Ad Litem," representatives of children's "best interest."

Since the inception of the Juvenile Justice System in this country at the beginning of the Twentieth Century, dealing with delinquency and family issues by the Justice System has been both controversial and challenging.

Perhaps the most constant source of migraines for those of us in the field of Juvenile Justice has been the "Status Offender."

A Status Offender is a Juvenile who, although not chargeable with "Delinquency" (criminal acts), yet is "Incorrigible" (behaviorally unmanageable for parents, school personnel, et al.) or is a constant runaway. The word "Status" in this instance means that the accused person is less than the age of majority, or, legally not an adult.

During my Rookie years, the fate of a juvenile declared "Incorrigible" was seldom different from those declared "Delinquent." This meant that the various States' Departments of Juvenile Corrections could be, and often was, overloaded with "Inkys;" some of whom had never, at any time, been charged with a criminal, or "Delinquent," act. In other words, it was as easy, nay, often easier, to be committed to a Juvenile State Prison Facility for not minding one's parents as for burglary, auto theft, and robbery.

Parents, school staff, social workers, Probation Officers would complain to Judges that they'd "Tried Everything" and that "Nothing Works." By the time some children in this category had been committed to a State's Department Of Corrections, the juvenile often had been in foster homes, psychiatrists' offices and placed on psychotropic drugs (Ritalin has been the Drug Of Choice for children for decades); they'd been in and out of schools, in and out of detention facilities, in and out of Residential Treatment Centers (Boys' and Girls' "Ranches"); all to no avail.

What the hell is wrong with that kid, anyway?

# THE DRAMA TRIANGLE

Ask any veteran Officer what, if any, call from Police Dispatch can invoke more caution and consternation in one's professional psyche than that of a family disturbance call. The answer you receive will likely be: "None!" Statistically, few other calls can present a greater likelihood of an officer being injured.

I believe most families that make this desperate call do so only once, possibly twice, in the family history. There are, however, some family units who, through their family problems, have come to know Police and Probation Officers on a first name, long-term, basis. These families are often referred to as: "The Friday Night Smiths."

There are almost as many catalysts for verbal and physical violence within family structures as there are families. For this reason, no Officer should make blanket assumptions as to what he or she is likely to encounter when going to a family residence. This is true even when – and sometimes, especially when – there is no apparent crisis, i.e., a routine house call being made by a Probation Officer or by a Social Worker.

The unique nature of each family's issues notwithstanding, investigating Caseworkers often do find some commonality in complaints stated by family members: alcoholism and/or drug abuse, sex (too much/too little), employment, or lack thereof, outside lovers, behaviors of their children.

What needs to be kept in mind at all times is that the stated complaints made by family members may have no relationship with the actual problems they are experiencing. So it usually is in "INKY" cases brought before the Juvenile Court.

No, it is <u>not</u> always the parents' fault! No, It is <u>not</u> always the kids' fault!

And it damn sure is not "Society's Fault!" The "fault" will always be found as being a combination of issues and events within the families and children's histories that can ultimately culminate in a family uproar. And some families get so caught up in the drama they become dependent upon the Dysfunction Drama itself to hold the family unit together. For example, observe, if you will, the stereotypical "Saturday Night Smiths:" Dad comes home late at night, drunk, slaps the wife and kids around, gets vile with the cops when they arrive; Dad is then handcuffed, and the wife goes for a cop's gun because now she is upset with her erstwhile rescuers and she doesn't want Dad jailed. Or, the teenager comes home, drunk and/or stoned, late at night and responds to parental inquires with a "fuck you!" and with a fist through the living room drywall.

Regardless of the causes of individual and family dysfunction, those families who decide, consciously or not, as a unit, to maintain destructive behaviors rather than face and deal with their genuine issues, do so in a way that has become sufficiently universal that the term "Drama Triangle" was created specifically for them. For example, during the 1970s, psychologist Eric Berne wrote several excellent books on this subject; I strongly recommend them ("Games People Play;" et al.) to any serious student of aberrant and destructive human behavior patterns.

Briefly, to make a Drama Triangle function, there are usually three Positions in a Game: the Prosecutor, the Victim 8land the Rescuer.

Any number of persons in the family (or other scenes, e.g., the workplace, a fraternity, etc.) can play destructive Games and become involved in a Drama Triangle. All that is required from the beginning is a solemn, unspoken, promise on the part of all players that no one will attempt to deal with actual problems the group may be pretending to deal with. Also, Drama Positions (Victim, Rescuer, Prosecutor) can be shifted from Player to Player at will, so that as actions and emotions play on, the Rescuer may become the Victim, Victim may become Prosecutor… these role shifts are a major dynamic of The Game.

Again, although Player's Roles may shift, this is done only to continue, indeed, intensify, the Game. Roles are never shifted to stop the Game and deal with real issues.

If/when outside intervention occurs, the players will more likely attempt to invite the outsider to take on a Game Role than to immediately and willingly engage in positive change.

When faced with a genuine crisis, the Players will need to have a "Bad Guy" upon whom they can heap the blame for all the family woes. It is not unusual, for reasons, which those with a working understanding of the Drama Triangle quickly identify, that the person identified to the Police as the Bad Guy by family members will be one of the children. And, more likely than not, the identified Bad Guy will willingly help the family set him or her up for the title and the fall. This person often is eventually identified as the "Incorrigible Child."

Police, Probation Officers, Lawyers, Judges – all need to deal with these families with firmness and total openness and honesty from the outset, lest they be unwittingly sucked into the family Game as well. Indeed, over the decades I witnessed as well countless therapists and staff members of Residential Treatment Centers fall into this trap. Dealing with disturbed persons---and particularly those who do not want to change (as is often the case with Court-Ordered clients, and/or those who are in therapy as a consequence of pressure from Various Significant Others)---is NEVER a "walk through the park."

# TAKE MY KID---PLEASE!

When a Court Officer enters into the initial exchange with people who are in trouble, the Officer must be honest. In particular, the Officer needs to fully spell out the strengths and the weaknesses of the Court System as applied in their case, and without exaggeration in any direction.

The "Incorrigible Families" I found easiest to deal with were those who would loudly <u>demand</u> upfront that we of the Court System "do something"---and they already knew from the beginning what they wanted that "something" to be done to "cure" their kid. The more upfront they were with their demands for detention, placement in a foster setting of some sort, psychiatric hospitalization, the easier it was to address every demand with what could and could not be possible within the Juvenile Justice System. In my experience, a little firm and upfront education went a long way with these families, and very often in the end they could be referred to Court – sponsored Family Counseling.

The difficult families were those folks who were masters of "I've Got A Secret." These folks will heap upon you gratitude and praise for helping and immediately go to work to undermine your every effort. Then they will bitch about you to the Judge. Probation Officers are not the only targets of these families. I have watched any number of Cops, Public Defenders and family counselors left swinging in the wind by angry family members during Court hearings . . .

Suffice it to say that few working within the Legal System like to deal with INKY families. During the late 1970s, the Chief of my Probation Department saw that Status Offenders, without exception, took up most of the time and energy on any Probation Officer's caseload. Therefore, he decided to separate Delinquency cases from Status Offender cases, so that, at least hypothetically, no Probation Officer would have to deal with both at the same time. This change did greatly enhance our ability to work with either category of juvenile and family.

Because the demands of working with families of Status Offenders are so consuming of one's time and emotional equilibrium, Status Offender caseloads were smaller in number, often by four-to-one. Still, most Officers greatly preferred the numerically larger Delinquency and Criminal Caseloads to the smaller, "INKY" Caseloads. In the beginning of this changeover, the Chief handpicked his Status Offender Caseload Officers.

By this time a major legal shift occurred in terms of options for dealing with non-delinquent children. The Supreme Court set new and highly specific guidelines for justifying the detention of any juvenile, and those guidelines were not generally easy to meet. Moreover, it was no longer permissible to commit a Status Offender to a State Department Of Corrections, when the juvenile was not Adjudicated (Found Guilty) of a Delinquency charge.

These changes surprised quite a few people working within the Juvenile Justice System, although child defense attorneys and child welfare advocates had been demanding them for years. Perhaps one of the more glaring cases demonstrating the need for this change was that of a twelve-year-old boy who with NO Delinquency adjudication priors, was committed to a Juvenile State Corrections Facility in the late '70s. There, he got into an altercation with a staff member, allegedly a relative of the Warden of that Facility; was charged with Aggravated Assault, was then, still, age twelve tried as an adult, convicted, and sentenced to seven years in that State's Adult Prison!

Now, more than ever, a dramatic increase in resources for Status Offenders, that is, Incorrigible/runaway, but not Delinquent, juveniles and their families, as needed. Now, more than ever, dramatic increases in Courts' budgets were needed as well, to pay for these services.

Now, forty years later, the Courts are still woefully short of funds and other resources for both Juvenile and Adult Probation Services. And, at least in Cordova City, much to the delight of Developers, the population continues to grow rapidly. The newcomers to this State are bringing their problems with them. What are we going to do about it?

## THEY STICK AROUND

INKYS and their parents tend to be needy and demanding people. If cops and P.O.'s allow it, these folks will quickly become very dependent upon the Badges and the Courts to make all things "better" for them, no matter how much of a mess family members make of things. And, of course, the family will always be ready to demonstrate its expertise in sabotage.

On the direction of the family Pastor, Susie Youngblood's mother transported her daughter to our Eastside Detention Facility as an Incorrigible Child. As I had become one of the "Chosen Ones" to serve in the Status Offender unit, the case fell to me.

Susie was a pretty fourteen-year-old girl with a winning smile and a tendency to strongly speak her mind whenever she desired. Her adoptive mother told me Susie had been shoplifting (no one called the police, she said), Susie had been ditching school, Susie had taken to lying and Susie was sneaking suggestive, skimpy clothing, assumedly shoplifted, into her school backpack and changing into those clothes in the school restroom. This latter allegation in particular disturbed Susie's mother the most: the family religion demanded fully covering and modest clothing on women and girls, so that, so Susie's mother told me, no male would get excited, lose control of self, and commit a rape.

Susie was unimpressed with her mother's concern. She denied shoplifting, admitted ditching and lying to her mother, and insisted that clothing she "borrowed from friends" was not suggestive but in style; the clothing her mother wanted her to wear, Susie said, went out of style in 1870.

What did Susie's mother want from us? She wanted Susie detained, just for a few days, just to teach a lesson.

Her Pastor had promised that we would do this upon mother's request.

When I let mama know her pastor did not have control over our Detention Facility and that Susie was not going to stay with us, both ladies were disappointed. Nevertheless, leave us they did.

The next weekend did find Susie residing in Detention. As she explained it to me, she was determined to show her mother what a jerk she (mother) was, so she did go to a mall, blatantly shoplifted, and when Police were called, she created an Emmy-winning scene, resulting in Detention, and also in a charge of assaulting an officer.

In Court Monday morning, Susie's mother made it clear that the whole affair was the P.O.'s fault: had I only detained Susie when the Pastor said I should, none of this would have happened.

Susie was placed on Probation. After reading reports describing the family dynamics, the Judge ordered that Susie be supervised on a Status Offender Caseload. In brief, the family issues involved mother, married first to an embezzler, the second time to a jewel thief, and now to an unemployed, bipolar religious fanatic who enjoyed reading the Bible for hours at a time: an older daughter, who was constantly quarreling with everyone and the youngest daughter, the Family Princess. Mother would complain about her husband privately to Susie, and then demand that the two visit the Pastor and pray about it. Susie would rebel and run out of the house. Mother would rush to the Pastor's office, and then her husband would accuse the mother of having an affair with the Pastor. Then he would read a lot from the bible.

When Susie learned that her being on Probation was not going to change her family's behavior, she ran away. When she was found and returned to Cordova City, she convinced the Court that she would continue to run away, so the Judge placed her in a girls' residential facility. This left Susie's mother faced with the need to face the issues in the marriage. She decided it would be easier instead to demand that the Court return Susie to the family home. Susie resolved that issue by running from the girls' Residential Facility. Fed up with all this, at last, the Judge returned Susie to her family home.

From that point, week after week, mother would call to complain about Susie. Susie would call to complain about her mother. Finally, at last, Susie turned eighteen years of age and therefore was no longer our responsibility.

She did go out on her own but would call still me periodically to complain about her mother calling her to complain about her bipolar stepfather.

Mother would also call me periodically, to complain about Susie not keeping in touch with her, and also to complain about her bipolar husband.

After a period of time, it seemed like a century, both gave up on me. However, I did not celebrate: when one of these family groups departs, another is certain to replace it.

# THE PROFESSIONAL PARENTS

She was a beautiful, very wealthy, wild, and party-going, sixteen-year-old girl. She had a mean streak and, when challenged, she would bring it out. When, one night following a beer party, she ran a red light and broadsided some Commoner's lowly Ford Taurus with her daddy's Mercedes, the Police cited her for running the red light and for not having a valid drivers license. She told the Citing Officer to go screw himself, tore up the citations, and threw them at the Officer. The Officer decided to bring her to Juvenile Detention and let her parents pick her up.

When the parents arrived they demanded that their daughter be detained as an Incorrigible Child. Her father told the Detention Intake Officer that if she were to be released, there'd be hell to pay because he was a friend of the Presiding Judge. To the Officer's credit, he sent the girl home anyway, with the very angry parents.

It did turn out that the girl's father knew our Presiding Judge. The father was a very wealthy attorney, and politically powerful in Cordova City; the mother was a very wealthy psychiatrist. The family resided in a million-dollar home on top of a hill overlooking Cordova City. The father took it upon himself to draw up an Incorrigible Child Petition against his daughter and then demanded that the Prosecutor's Office take her through the Juvenile Court System. The Chief Prosecutor did as he was told; the girl was adjudicated Incorrigible, and then she was assigned to my caseload.

I made an appointment for a home visit. I drove my motorcycle onto their driveway; the walled and gated home was easily 150 yards in from the street. I noticed that the garage was itself larger than my own home. I parked my motorcycle, walked up to the twelve-foot tall double doors at the home's entrance, and knocked.

The girl opened the door. I introduced myself and explained that I needed to obtain information for my report to the Court. The girl said: "Get it from them," pointing to her parents, both of which were present. Then she left the area.

I introduced myself to the parents. At that time, the Mother psychiatrist said to Father's attorney: "You answer his questions. You're the one who gives her anything she wants!"

The father replied: "Don't you put this crap on my desk!"

Mother psychiatrist, cleverly coining a new phrase, shot back with: "If the shoe fits, wear it!"

The attorney picked up a nearby table lamp and dashed it to the ground, saying to the psychiatrist, "The next one goes on your head!"

The psychiatrist said, "You just try it, and after you get up off the floor, I'll let the Police take you away."

I quickly excused myself and left.

A few days later, my Supervisor told me that Mrs. Psychiatrist had scheduled me to attend staffing that afternoon at the local Psychiatric Center. Mrs. Psychiatrist, it so happened, was also a board member at that Hospital and had arranged for her daughter's admission as a patient.

As I walked into the waiting area outside the hospital's conference room, I heard the parents screaming at each other. A few hospital staff members were present, doing what they could to usher in a return to calm. The parents saw me enter the conference room, stopped shouting, and sat down.

The staffing was short and was and a rubber stamp of what Mrs. Psychiatrist had already decided. The daughter remained hospitalized.

I walked out into the hospital parking lot toward my motorcycle. I heard loud voices. Several parked vehicles from where I stood were Mr. Attorney and Mrs. Psychiatrist, resuming their shouting match where they had left off just before their daughter's staffing. Once again, the hospital staff was running out of the parking lot to restore peace.

Mrs. Psychiatrist slapped Mr. Attorney. Mr. Attorney slapped Mrs. Psychiatrist. I started up my motorcycle and left.

Several days afterward, I received a Court Order, releasing the hospitalized daughter from my Caseload, and further Court responsibility.

Thanks be to God.

# ALCOHOLICS

Anyone reading this book and not getting the idea that alcoholism and drug addiction is seen a lot by workers within the Criminal Justice System has missed a major issue. Please go back to Chapter One and begin again.

At the same time, please do not infer that alcohol and drugs "cause" criminal behavior. If that were true, imagine how many millions of Margarita drinking criminals would be pillaging your neighborhoods tonight. I have never met a person who had once been a totally law abiding-citizen, but who had innocently ingested alcohol or drugs and found himself helpless, with no choice but to commit robbery, burglary, auto theft, rape, or any other sort of destruction and mayhem.

Indeed, people who abuse these substances often do stupid and dangerous things to themselves and others. It is also true that people who do not abuse these substances often do stupid and dangerous things to themselves and others. The behavior of drunks and druggies is especially horrible for sober people to have to deal with. Watching substance abusers destroy themselves and others is sad and frustrating at best. Have you ever been to a drinking party where you were the only sober person in the crowd? That was fun, wasn't it?

This does not, however, demonstrate that substance abuse "creates" crime. People, and their stupid and destructive decisions, create crime. Being stoned or drunk does not create, out of anywhere, criminal thought in a heretofore criminally thought-free brain. Drugs and alcohol create destructive human behavior like cars create accidents.

Sadly, when substance abusers are run through the Criminal Justice System, and when confronted regarding their behavior, they will blame it all on the drugs and the booze. Although they will verbalize a desire for change, few will be willing to do what is necessary to deal with their issues, including substance abuse. What they will be hoping for is that the P.O. or the Therapist will somehow change everything for them.

Typical of the human misery I would see in alcoholic families is the case of an "Inky" fifteen year-old-girl on my Caseload who lived with her thirty-six-year-old mother and with her mother's live-in boyfriend. Mother had never been gainfully employed; she was, she told me, "disabled" in some way or another, and she collected some sort of monthly Government financial assistance. Mother's boyfriend allegedly drove trucks on occasion in order to bring a few more dollars into the home.

Both mother and boyfriend were alcoholic. The boyfriend was one of the "Saturday Night Smiths' I've mentioned earlier: A late-night drunk, he typically returned home to beat on his girlfriend; she'd call the Police---in this case, by the time the Police arrived, the now-hysterical daughter would also, be verbally and physically acting out. Most often, as a result, the daughter, not the boyfriend, would be arrested and jailed.

This Game pattern was sufficiently predictable that I finally decided to drive by the family trailer and visit each Friday evening, with the hope that this would help to prevent the Friday night blow-ups. During my initial visits, mother, daughter, boyfriend, and I would discuss family issues of the week and their problems in general.

This went on for six weeks. However, there was no visible improvement in anyone's behavior.

Following the weekend after my sixth home visit, the boyfriend called me at my office to tell me that if I ever came by trailer again, he'd kick my ass (his words). In the background, I heard the daughter, my Probationer, shout, "Mike, shut up! Don't mess with my P.O., he's a Black Belt!" Mike shouted back, "You shut up! He ain't no Black Belt!" then he asked me "You a Black Belt?" I responded, "Yes." The boyfriend hung up on me.

The Friday after my conversation with the boyfriend, I appeared at the trailer. As I parked my bike, I watched the boyfriend run out the back door of the trailer, enter his truck, and drive off. Mother walked out of the front door toward me. Still seated on my motorcycle, I greeted her.

I asked her what was going on with the boyfriend's quick departure. She replied: "He's afraid of you. He called your Supervisor and she told Mike that you're a Black Belt. So I told him I was going to tell you to kick his ass if he hit me or my daughter again."

"Why don't you just kick him out?" I asked, and I immediately regretted saying it. I knew from my Pre-Sentence Investigation that mother has experienced innumerable "revolving door" boyfriends over the years. All were like Mike. The next one most likely would be the same.

The woman replied, "Look at me. I'm thirty-six years old, and I look sixty. Who else is going to want me?"

Shortly following that visit, I transferred into the Detention Division and created the Department's Juvenile

Detention Officers Academy. I will bet that nothing ever changed in that family. I hope that the boyfriend, Mike, believed my replacement on the caseload was also a Black Belt. I did advise mama to tell Mike so, whether true or not.

# EMANCIPATION

Over the decades I have heard both natural and adoptive parents loudly proclaim "I'm gonna EMANCIPATE him/her and let him/her hit the bricks! And I don't give a DAMN what happens!" Hundreds of times over my years as a Probation Officer have these words echoed in my presence, both in-office and at family residences.

Strictly speaking, the "Emancipation" of a minor is a legal activity that requires formal Court action. If "Emancipation" is ordered by the Court, this allows a person not yet of the State's legal "age of majority," to go their own way, no longer legally responsible to the parents, and vice versa.

The process of legal Emancipation differs from State to State, although some states have no statutes at all allowing Emancipation of a minor child. For example, some states in the recent past have lowered their Statutory recognition of the age of a person's majority from age twenty-one, to age eighteen. Prior to that change, when twenty-one was the legally recognized age of majority, upon application to the Court, the Court had sometimes allowed Emancipation at age eighteen. However, when some States had changed their age of majority from twenty-one to eighteen, there was no provision written in the law allowing for the setting of another, lower, the age for Emancipation.

During my career, when the question comes of Emancipation came up, I had to respond that my State no longer had a statute allowing for it. Not one desperate, angry, frustrated parent wanted to believe me. I've been called a liar more times than I can remember over this, by numerous parents and therapists, as well as by a few surprisingly uninformed attorneys.

How does the typical, desperate, citizen usually go about researching the Emancipation Statues, or for that matter, nearly any other Law? Rather than ask a Lawyer (they cost a lot of money, and what the hell do they know, anyway?), he/she asks a friend, who has a cousin, who knows someone who works at a fast-food establishment, who once served a guy who is a cop in Ottawa, who told him that the Law regarding (you fill in the blank) is <u>exactly</u> what the citizen wanted the Law to be in the first place. Come on, folks, if you need legal advice, ask a Lawyer.

*Chapter IV*

# SOME HIGHLIGHTS FROM THE FIELD

## INTRODUCTION:

Here is a secret to being a successful field officer: regardless of the socio-economic character of the community, become a part of the community. Be prepared to discover that we are all more similar than dissimilar. This chapter will provide some examples.

# ZACK

It was a dark and stormy night. No, really: unusual though it is for Cordova City, located as it is in a desert setting, it was a <u>dark and stormy night!</u>

An Indian Reservation Police Officer caught in his headlights a new red Mercedes sports car pulling out from a residence where a car newer than 1970 would be a rarity, much less a new red Mercedes sports car. The Officer checked the Mercedes out through his on board computer: the car was hot. The officer's Visibar lights went on. The Mercedes accelerated; the chase was on.

The Mercedes departed "the Rez" and entered Cordova City, where it was joined by a trailing group of Cordova City Police cars. The Mercedes rode on, occasionally at speeds over one hundred miles per hour.

The hot Mercedes was joined by a dozen more Police cars and also by a Police rotary-winged aircraft. On the one hand, it was fortunate that since the time was one A.M., few other cars were on the street. On the other hand, the downpour of rain was hard and constant, and the streets were slick.

At last, the driver of the Mercedes took a bad turn and ended up in a residential cul-de-sac. The Police blocked the area with their cars. The airborne Police centered their spotlight on the hot car.

The driver exited the Mercedes and ran. Several Police Officers gave a foot chase. One, Officer Tony Sparkman, caught up with the driver, tackled him, rolled with him in the mud, at last, handcuffed him and, while reciting to the driver the "Miranda warnings," Officer Sparkman turned the driver over so they were face-to-face.

The driver was Officer Sparkman's oldest son, Zack.

While engaged in my Pre-Sentence Investigation of this case, I met with Officer Tony Sparkman at a restaurant, for coffee and conversation. Tony recounted for me the incredibly frightening felony pursuit and the capture of his son. Tears came to the veteran Cop's eyes as he said: "I still can't believe it. I can't believe it was my son. What are the odds? What are the odds?"

Sad but true, daddy carrying a Badge, or being a member of the State Bar, or even being a Judge, does not award a Mantle of Immunity from disaster to the family. My various Caseloads have seen juveniles with all these authority figures, and more, as parents: teachers, high-ranking corporate executives, elected officials; I promise you, no one is immune. Yes, even in my own family there were problems. One day, while in a deep funk over the behavior of my sons, I recall a Judge saying to me "Kurt, have you ever heard the one about the preacher's daughter is the biggest sinner in town?"

The point is those of us who have been among the more economically and socially fortunate in life often like to believe that problems with children and crime happen only to those "Po' Folk; the "Trailer Trash," the "Minorities." Not true: these problems are evenly spread out over the entire spectrum of the human population. No one is immune. And, that awful telephone call at two a.m. can be truly humbling.

There is a "Zack" in everyone's family. This is not the end of the world. Deal with your own "Zack," not with anger, but with love in your heart for your kid.

## SUBPOENA TO SITKA

It was never clear to me how it was that a new, gorgeous, girlfriend would accompany my sixteen-year-old Probationer, Randy Horton, every week. Randy was short and stocky five feet four inches tall, easily one hundred eighty pounds, dark hair, thick black eyebrows, face heavily marked with Acne Vulgaris. He was a burglar and an auto thief. He did always had a major stash of pot hidden close by perhaps the Weed was the key to his successful love life….

When given a friendly greeting, Randy would flash a bright smile. He had a wonderful, if often devilish, sense of humor. He did have the ability to laugh at himself when he screwed up totally. When caught in a bad act, he was usually ready to admit his guilt upfront. Rarely did he seriously complain about whatever punishment would be meted out. This is not to say that he did not prefer to get away with no punishment, nor that he did not attempt to negotiate for mitigation of his punishment whenever possible.

But when the Judge said: "Randy, here it is," Randy would take without whining. I like this quality in an offender. Far too often we have to deal with the offender and attorney who trots in psychiatrists, Reverends, and others that the fault lies not so much with the offender, who is, in reality, a victim as well, but with all of us, and with our Sick Society.

Within the first six months of being on my probation caseload, Randy had been detained three times. He was visited, along with his parents, by young ladies far more often than by his attorney. He seemed to thrive in the Detention Facility. He charmed Detention Officers and Detention School Teachers, particularly the women. He garnered from Detention staff privileges often beyond those typically given to inmates, to the extent that at times the Detention Director would wonder aloud if paychecks would not be next for Randy.

For myself, the third time in jail was the charm. This time, Randy was in our Detention Facility without a prayer of release before his Sentencing Hearing, which would mostly mean a transfer to a State Corrections Facility.

During my first few months with Randy's case, his mother, who, incidentally, was a veteran of a number of relationships with abusive drunk boyfriends, would verbally express her belief that I too must be a drunk and a womanizer. After all, aren't all men drunks and womanizers? And I (gasp!) ride a motorcycle, which proves that I'm no good! Her boyfriend didn't like me, either; he was certain that I was trying to "score " with Randy's mother.

At last, and I suppose it was because Randy had been ordered into Detention for the third time and I was making a Big Thing out of it, mother decided to converse civilly with me. Now, she had a wonderful tale to tell of her brother, Randy's uncle, being employed "in construction" on an island in Alaska. She suggested that we consider sending Randy to live on this remote Alaskan island with his uncle. After all, how much trouble can a guy working on houses on an island up around the Arctic Circle get into? Think, she suggested, of how much money this would save our State's taxpayers.

Think, also, that if he stayed in our State and was to be sent to a State Corrections Facility, Randy would be out on parole soon enough; what then for Randy and the community?

Randy's Public Defender liked the idea of Randy being sent to Alaska. I liked the idea. The Judge liked the idea as well and lost no time in ordering me to arrange for Randy to live in Alaska. Consequently, Randy was residing with his uncle in Alaska before I drank my next morning's pot of coffee.

Some four months later, I received a Subpoena from the District Court in Sitka, Alaska. The District Judge in Sitka had decided that a representative of our Court needed to appear in person and explain to him where we got off, sending our criminals to his State. Accordingly, he sent the Subpoena for me to appear before him, along with a two-way ticket for me on Alaska Airlines (nice, but I would have far preferred a cruise ship) and vouchers for a hotel room, meals, and various other expenses. It seems that Randy and his Uncle had been charged with several residential burglaries.

During my four-day stay, I saw Sitka, Ketchikan, and Kodiak Island. I was wined and dined by the District

Attorney, the Public Defender, and the Court's Probation Officer (at that time, she was being paid by the State of Alaska more than double my wage). Following a strong admonition directed my way from the Alaskan Court to keep our Criminal Trash out of Alaska, I left Sitka with Randy in tow. I also left with three frozen Chinook salmon, courtesy of the local Cannery.

Randy's Uncle was sent to a California prison, courtesy of the Alaskan taxpayers: he was convicted of one burglary by way of a plea negotiation. Alaska at the time possessed no prisons. Alaskan Courts sent their convicts to California prisons, through a compact with that state.

Less than thirty days following our return from Alaska, Randy elected to conduct a midnight burglary of a business. Cordova City Police arrived at the scene quickly, because Randy'd triggered an alarm. A struggle between Randy and Police Officers ensued, and when Randy broke free and ran, an officer struck him with a fatal gunshot.

Not everyone's story will have a happy ending. And, sometimes a bad saga can unexpectedly continue and become even worse. The Police Officer who shot Randy was killed three weeks later; he was broad-sided at a traffic intersection by a drunk who ran a red light.

# MINT TEA

Billy Dietrich was on my Probation Caseload, having been found guilty of possession of Marijuana. No sooner had his file settled on my desk than it was topped with a notice that Billy was in detention on a new charge: Possession of Marijuana, once again.

I walked nearly sixty meters from my office to the Detention Facility. I entered the cell block in which Billy was languishing. There, I met my new, clearly unhappy, Probationer.

I said, "You Billy Dietrich?" "Yes, Sir."

"Billy, I'm your P.O. My name is Kurt Niemann." "Yes, Sir."

"Billy, what's going on here?"

"Sir - - -"

"Billy, "Kurt" will do. I was an Enlisted Man once."

My cheap attempt at humor was lost on the kid. He was fearful of the possible outcome of his situation.

I said, "Billy, the ink wasn't dry on the Judge's Order placing you on Probation, and here you are, in here on yet another Marijuana charge."

"But, Sir, it wasn't weed. It was Mint Tea." "Billy - - - "

"Honest to God, Sir, it was Mint Tea."

I read to Billy excerpts from the Police Officer's report. The report chronicled how two Cordova City Police Officers observed Billy Dietrich walking Eastbound on Arapaho Road, not far from his parent's apartment, a plastic baggie in his hand. The Officers shouted for Billy to stop. Billy ran.

The Officers gave chase; while running, Billy was observed to be stuffing the contents of the baggie into his mouth and attempting to swallow. An Officer tackled Billy and dropped him on the sidewalk. The other Officer placed two fingers into Billy's mouth and scooped the green leafy substance remaining in Billy's mouth out, and placed the remains back into the confiscated plastic baggie. Billy was arrested and detained; the green leafy substance was sent to the Police crime lab. Lab test reports were still pending.

"Mint Tea, Billy?"

"Yes, Sir, honest to God, Sir - - -" "Why did you run, Billy?"

"Sir, I had just gone into a store, bought the tea, walked out of the store, and the next thing, the cops are chasing me. I knew they'd think it was weed, so I ran."

"And you tried to eat it - - -"

"So they couldn't find nothin', then I wouldn't be charged with nothin'."

"So, okay, Billy, if it wasn't weed, just mint tea- - -" "I know, Sir, it was stupid. But it was mint tea."

"Okay, Billy. See you in Court in the morning."

"'Night, Sir."

There was no Court in the morning. The lab report showed Billy Dentrich had been, willfully and knowingly, in possession of - - - Mint Tea.

# I STEAL, YOU STEAL - - -

He was on Probation; He'd been found guilty of burglary. Now, he was detained once again, on a new charge of burglary.

At his Arraignment Hearing, he pled Not Guilty. He told me that he did do the burglary. The Police said that they initially contacted him at a routine traffic stop. However, They found his car to be loaded with stereo gear and records. This loot was quickly tied into the burglary only a few hours earlier.

Defendants have pled Not Guilty to far more serious charges, under far more incriminating circumstances. There is any number of reasons for an accused person to do this, many of them legitimate. For example, the arresting process may be tainted. The chain of evidence may be broken. Witnesses may be mistaken or lying. Or, here's one for you: The guy may be innocent!

So, what happened with my detained burglar? He was found guilty (as he should have been) by consequence of a plea negotiation, and later, he found his way to a berth with the State Department of Corrections. As we prepared him for his transport to the State Facility, he looked up at me and said, "this is bogus, Neimann."

"Okay, so why is this bogus?" "I didn't steal noting'!"

"Dude! Your car was loaded with stolen loot!" "Bullshit! All that was MY stuff."

"You were just storing it at the other guy's house, right?"

"Dammit, that stuff was all mine! I just didn't know it was until I got it all in my car! All that shit was stolen from me, a year ago. So I ain't guilty of stealing nothin'! I just got my stuff back! This is a bogus rap!"

So, seems that he only stole his stuff back, sort of like rotating community property: I steal, you steal…

# OFFICE CAPERS

Professors of Business Administration can explain far better than I why Executive Level positions seem to expand faster than the numbers of staff in the lower ranks seem to justify. Over the years I have come to believe this is done so that the upper ranks will have plenty of middle ranks available to take the heat for upper-rank screwups.

At one time, our upper-level leadership decided that yet one more Division and Division Director was needed. Hired was a man I elected to nickname (out of his earshot, of course) "The Chief Shrink." This man held an MBA and a Ph.D. in psychology. He had formerly been employed in one of the major Psychiatric Hospitals in New York. This man slavishly adhered to the "Medical Model" in every last nitpicky manner possible. "Medical Model" was at the time the latest academic buzzword adopted by the Criminal Justice System. This line of thought held that an offender is not a Bad Guy, he is "sick." The sickness causing the person to commit a crime could be the result of almost any kind of trauma in life. This "sickness" could be cured through treatment, rather than punishment.

"Chief Shrink" believed that if offenders were to be properly "treated," the Criminal Justice Agency buildings must be thought of as Criminal Justice "Clinics." Therefore, he set about to change how we conducted business. The first item to leave us was the Probation Building telephone operator's P.A. system. We must,

Chief Shrink decreed, have nearly total silence within our buildings.

Conversations between Officers were forbidden within the building, except for in Courtrooms and the executive offices. Dictation of Reports was permitted so long as this was done behind a closed office door.

All employees except Executives were to go to the telephone operator's station to check for their messages, which the hapless Operator was now handwriting by the bushel. All office doors were to be closed at all times. There was to be no talking in the hallways. Talking in offices between occupying Officers was forbidden as well. "Chief Shrink" commissioned our maintenance staff to create fifty partitions, six feet high by eight feet in length, all on rollers, to be placed between the one hundred Officers' desks. The belief was: if they can't see each other, they're not likely to speak with each other. To discourage us from moving the partitions, "Chief Shrink" would appear at random times, throwing open office doors, as though to say: "Gotcha!"

Some Officers anonymously protested "Chief Shrink's" preposterous behavior. For example, from time to time all the office partitions were found in the hallways in the morning. A few partitions appeared in his office. Telephone messages by the ream were written and delivered to him, most of them bogus. Officers would leave their office doors open, then depart and call themselves, so that "Chief Shrink" could be seen running out of his office, taking the Officer's telephone off the hook, and then slamming the Officer's door closed.

Officers were forbidden to verbally communicate with "Chief Shrink." Communication was accomplished by written memos only. Replies to replies to memos always needed photocopies of all other prior memos and replies attached to them as well.

One morning, "Chief Shrink" entered his office and discovered his chair missing. He searched all the offices in the building; no chair. Soon, his Secretary announced that she'd found his chair, in the staff ladies restroom, with a note attached saying: "Greetings From The Phantom!"

For whatever reason, "Chief Shrink" decided I had done this dastardly deed. He stormed into my office, face beet-red, and screamed, professionally, of course, his outrage toward me. I sat and listened, realizing that denial would be futile. I had not been the "Bad Guy" in this particular event.

And, I had no idea who the culprit was. Those who did know did not disclose the perpetrator's name to me until nearly ten years later. It seems that the perp had sworn them all to silence until he finally left the agency.

The second "Chair" event was at the same time both comic and sad! Again, "Chief Shrink's" chair was missing; this time, as it later turned out, forever. No one knew, or, at least, admitted to knowing, who had the chair. One afternoon following the chair's disappearance, I walked into my office, to see "Chief Shrink" lying on his back, under my chair, suit on body, pen, and pad in hands. He told me he was looking for the County sticker with a serial number attached to my chair. I said, "Excuse me," and left for another hour.

Ultimately, "Chief Shrink" had listed in his notebook every serial number of every office chair in the Agency. He then searched County records to discover which chair had been assigned to which office. To his dismay, "Chief Shrink" discovered that when the Probation offices were furnished, no records of chair serial numbers were made. The man was now beside himself. He all but disappeared, first from our view, then from his office, and, finally, the building. Shortly afterward, He left the agency.

I've been told that "Chief Shrink" returned to his natural habitat: a hospital setting, once again, in New York.

# DEBBIE

Most often when Debbie Newcomb was detained, the nine-year-old girl would give her name to the Police as that of one of her brothers. Being just a tiny, towheaded little kid, the cops would generally believe her.

The male Detention Intake Officer's strip search, however, would determine that the little girl had lied to the Officers. Of course, female Detention Officers would be immediately called in to complete the search and booking process. Mistakes of this sort are not all that rare, although the subject being searched and discovered to be of the opposite gender most often is a male homosexual prostitute, dressed as a woman.

In case you're wondering, most states' statutes provide that no child less than the age of eight years can be charged with a "Delinquent" (criminal) act. The law does not prevent, therefore, the detention, on charges of Delinquent behavior, of children eight years of age and older.

Debbie was detained on a charge of Attempted Homicide. The victim, in this case, was a Police Officer who responded to a shoplifting call at a grocery market. When approached by the Officer, screaming and struggling Debbie pulled a straight razor from her jeans pocket and severely slashed the Police Officer multiple times.

Debbie resided with her mother and three brothers in a trailer park near that grocery store. The four children in this family each had a different father, all, whereabouts and names unknown, at least to the State. The three older brothers had been administered psychological evaluations by the elementary school district and were all found to be suffering varying levels of mental retardation. A few months before her detention, Debbie had also been tested and was found to have a full-scale I.Q. score of 63. All four siblings attended classes specifically offered by the school district to retarded children.

Through her Public Defender, Debbie entered a "Not Guilty" plea. At the Public Defender's motion, the Judge ordered me to schedule a psychological evaluation for Debbie: at that time, they were not yet aware, nor was I, tha the school district had already conducted one. I scheduled Debbie's psychological evaluation with our department's Lead Psychologist, a man who at the time had been with us more than twenty years. He was thorough; he was, in my experience, always on the money. His credentials regarding with delinquents and criminal offenders were unassailable.

As part of my routine in the event of a court-ordered "Psych-Eval," I visited Debbie's school, to discover if there had been any prior behavior or academic problems with her within the school system. The school staff had learned earlier why Debbie had not been attending classes. The principal and Debbie's two assigned teachers begged me to keep this nine-year-old girl in Detention and out of their school. She was, they explained, a chronic creator of uproar in class and the recess yard. She would drive her classmates, all evaluated as retarded, into frenzied verbal and physical outbursts. How could such a seriously retarded child, they wondered, be so violently disposed of?

My first clue toward the answer to the schoolteacher's question came from my department's veteran psychologist: he reported that Debbie had achieved a Full-Scale I.Q. score on the Wechsler Test of 126!

So where did the Full-Scale number of "63," on her previous evaluation, compiled by the school district, come from? Before disclosing this latest score to an astonished school district, I'd learned that the testing psychologist who had conducted and reported on the "63" testing had also, earlier, conducted the evaluations on her three older brothers. After hearing of the results of my department's evaluation, no one in the school district offices or at the school was willing to talk to me. It didn't take a Sherlock Holmes to figure this one out. Then, upon hearing of the evaluation scores on Debbie, the Public Defender, clearly perceiving that his "she's retarded" defense plan was not going to fly nor float, sought to at least partially heal his wounds by demanding that I be removed from Debbie's case. And so I was. Deo Gracias!

Footnote: the Court eventually placed Debbie into a Residential Treatment Facility, where she remained until her eighteenth birthday. I was told that Debbie's behavior during her residence at the Center was atrocious more often than not. Those staff in the various group homes that devote so much time and energy to persons such as Debbie need, in my opinion, to be sainted.

# A SHOT HITS HOME

Six-year-old Jaime lived with his maternal grandparents. His nineteen-year-old mother (!) was living with her most recent boyfriend, somewhere in Cordova City. Jamie's maternal grandparents' residence was located six houses to the West of my own family.

Jamie, at age six, had a reputation of being "trouble" among parents of similarly aged children in my neighborhood. Consequently, he had few playmates that I can remember. His only companions seemed to be his rather extensive collection of B-B guns. When not at school, he was rarely seen without one of his guns. He shot at trees, at signs, at mailboxes, and occasionally at neighborhood cats. A number of neighbors would call the Police and, occasionally, the local Children's Services Office. Jamie being less than eight years of age, the Police decided they could do nothing.

Children's Services decided likewise. In short, nobody, except the neighbors, seemed to care.

Late one afternoon my ten-year-old son was riding his bicycle near Jamie's house. At that time, Jamie "accidentally" shot my son with a B-B gun. My son was struck in his right eye.

I was notified by the Police Officer who had responded to the 911 call by a neighbor. I drove immediately to the hospital emergency room to which my son had been taken. My son was very fortunate, considering: the B-B had not entered the eye itself; it had merely entered the eye socket, rotated around the eye socket a few times, and then it rested near the occipital nerve.

Two days after the shooting the B-B was removed. My medical insurance footed the bill. My son's eye was not seriously damaged.

Jamie's grandparents raised hell with the Police Department for confiscating Jaime's B-B gun. Astonishingly, the Police Department returned the gun to the grandparents.

To my total disgust, Children's Services, as usual, displayed no interest in this event or the state of Jamie's alleged parental supervision.

## SPEAKING OF SAINTS

Her sixteen-year-old son was a petty thief and on my Probation caseload. Her fifteen-year-old daughter was quiet, unassuming and a straight-A student in High School.

The father of her two children left her and the children before they were in kindergarten. He disappeared and child support money from him was not a possibility. She worked two jobs and went to school once her children were in elementary classes. Six years later, she was a Registered Nurse.

Her two children had different ways of dealing with their genetic history (mother, a blue-eyed blond; father, a black South African National): her son reacted to harassment from blacks and whites by fighting and by stealing; her daughter, by losing herself in books.

Mother was friendly and plain speaking. She was a spiritually oriented lady, and optimistic almost to a fault. The few times I spoke with her before I was transferred from that Caseload and into a different assignment, I was very impressed by her total demeanor and by the quality of her character.

This was particularly true considering her ability to deal positively with her full-time hospital assignment: she was a Pediatric I.C.U. Nurse.

During our last conversation, she revealed to me a few experiences with saving a few babies, and with babies dying in her arms. I have no idea how anyone can survive an hour of that kind of experience, much less her ten years. But, she told me she loved her job and intended to devote her career to Pediatric I.C.U. I believe that when she dies, Mother Theresa will be greeting her with open arms.

# DEFINITELY NOT JACKIE CHAN

If you've seen the first "Karate Kid" movie, in that story there was the large, muscled guy with a huge ego who ran a karate school; he was a bully and, in short, the very personification of Evil.

Just imagine that gentleman's karate school is located in your neighborhood. Well, my assigned area in Cordova City was blessed with a school operated by a man who could have been his twin. The guy running this school had three children in his family: two boys and a girl. All three siblings lived to fight, often, preferably by ambush and without provocation.

This man's daughter was on my Probation Caseload. This eighteen-year-old, one hundred fifty pound, package of anger, with violence on her mind at all times, preferred attacking and beating on girls but had no qualms about combat with boys as well. She had been a contestant with both sexes in local "Cage Fights." She usually won, but when she lost, few dared to face her wrath.

No surprise, then, that she had been found guilty on Assault charges – she had taken on two girls at a party and both went to E.R.; soon afterward, she was on my Probation Caseload.

Her two brothers, both older than my Probationer, had a unique way of marketing their father's karate school. They would frequent events where large crowds would be milling about, particularly sporting events, but large-scale flea markets and State and County fairs served their goals nicely as well. The brothers would choose a young person as their target, attack, beat the person mercilessly, and then place their school's business card on the victim's chest, saying, "If you want to learn how to protect yourself, you have to go to this school for training." Then, they would leave their victim, and, often, an astonished crowd as well. Seldom would Police be called and be present in time to intercept these acts? When Police did appear, the two brothers would split up and run into the crowds, meeting later at a pre-arranged locality.

When in his fighting prime, their father would enjoy assembling a group of his school's karate instructors, enter a bar and "clean it out."

These people are not Martial Artists; they are thugs. "Objectivity," whatever that means in real life, was next to impossible for me to maintain in dealing with this family. My goal became to dump this case on someone else. My supervisor was not sympathetic, nor was he cooperative. I was blessed with this case to the bitter end.

The "bitter end" occurred in a "cage fight" event in San Diego. According to court testimony, my Probationer handily won her match in short order.

However, she did not cease beating her erstwhile opponent, now her victim, until the other woman was to be forever a quadriplegic. My former Probationer did serve eight and one-half years in a California Penitentiary. I leave it to the reader to guess what she is like today.

Thousands of lives have been improved, even saved, through martial arts training. I can personally think of no better way for a young person to develop self-confidence, physical and mental skills, self-awareness, and respect for others. Most martial arts schools in this country will provide all this for young people and at a surprisingly reasonable cost. However, America's economy is, at least allegedly, based on Free Enterprise. There is no law forbidding the establishment of a lousy school. <u>caveat emptor</u>.

## NOT FRANK BUCK, EITHER

While we're on the subject of mindless violence conducted by mindless people, I feel compelled to relate yet another case of a father of a Probationer on my Caseload seemingly needing to go out of his way to violate all that I hold dear.

Yes, I will agree that <u>any</u> criminal act is, and should be, a violation of my values. Sex offenders, particularly child molesters, and wife beaters are way up there on my list. And just below those sorry people are the <u>wannabe</u> "Soldiers Of Fortune" and the "Big Game Hunters." These folks seem to go out of their way, often at wildly inappropriate times, to proclaim that they are the actual, genuine, professional, Big-Game-Hunter-Better-Than-Hemmingway article. Only those observers who are the least informed and least experienced in life will accept this drivel as "genuine." They will cause actual professional hunters and professional soldiers to hasten to the nearest commode to retch.

It happened that I was assigned the case of a family wherein the Head Of The Household, a former Citizen of the British Crown, definitely saw himself as a Big Game Hunter. Coincidentally, during that time I was periodically serving weekends as a volunteer Hunter Safely Instructor for our State's Game and Fish Department. It sometimes seems as though The Fates go out of their way to test my emotional equilibrium.

What this man did to cause me to recoil was his behavior during the Pre- Sentence Investigation period. When I made a telephone call to his home to arrange my initial interview, the man responded that I was to "Keep the hell off (his) property." I called the defense attorney, who of course was well aware that this man needed to co-operate. He asked me to set a date and told me that I should plan to find a more cooperative offender and family at that time.

Two days later, this guy called me and announced that if I did show at his home I would be shot. "I have lots of guns," He added. I assured him I would be there, with a few friends in uniform. He asked me, "Will they have guns?" Ah, those crazy Brits.

I did arrive at the offender's residence, with Cordova City's own Curly and his partner Brad. Before we exited our car, we noted two barking Dobermans on the front yard, standing between two large trees. Connected to the two trees was a steel cable. The two dogs' steel cable leashes were connected to the cable attached to the trees, giving the dogs a thirty-foot run by which they could guard the property.

Wishing that I had the Colt .45 I'd carried in the Corps when we exited our car my right hand went inside my jacket. Curly and Brad, in uniform at the time, had their holsters unsnapped.

Suddenly, one of the dogs broke loose from his restraining cable! We froze. Then, the loose dog sat down and was quiet. Curly advanced a few feet toward the residence. The dog remained in a seated position. Brad and I advanced. The dog slowly, silently, arose, then, walking, retreated to the far opposite end of the property, and, once again, sat, next to the other dog, which was lying in the grass, seemingly oblivious to our presence.

My new "client" appeared at the front door, threw a disgusted glance at the "guard dogs" and, however reluctantly, invited us inside.

Once inside this home, we observed seemingly endless "trophy" animal heads all along the walls of the living room and family room. There were several dozen species represented: deer, sheep, antelope, cats, on and on, each adorned with an engraved brass plate describing the kind of animal and the history of the kill.

But the most expressionless and forlorn head inside this home was that of The Head Of The Household's wife. Throughout the interview, I saw no emotion in her face. I did not hear her speak one word. He would bark orders her way; she would jump up and get his coffee, a document, whatever. Her eyes displayed a blank expression.

During this interview, the man found ways to make constant references to his trophies and his many firearms, all, save one, having calibers of no less than .30-06. He made two comments that I will never forget:

"Only pussies don't hunt." Then:

"All real men love to kill. We live to kill. It's in our blood, from back in caveman days."

The interview having at length been concluded, we three Officers arose and exited toward the front door. Then, placed by the front door, I noticed the one small-caliber firearm in the man's collection. It was a .22 pump action rifle. Seeing me notice this rifle, the man said: "It's loaded with birdshot.

When one of my dogs pisses me off I shoot him in the ass. They learn from that."

Leaving this home was a pure delight. I decided that in this country, the Liberal Senators are not the only enemies of the Second Amendment to the United States Constitution. People like this man can do more damage to those of us who depend on our Right To Bear Arms than can a thousand Ted Kennedy or George Soros types.

## CURLY VI

While on routine patrol (here we go again…), I received a radio call to take a burglary complaint. Upon arrival, the complaining party met me at the door to the home. He was an elderly man. We went to the dining room, where we had a view of his backyard. I proceeded to ask him routine questions to fill out the report.

To my surprise I observed a fourteen-year-old boy, climbing over the fence, into the old man's backyard. I asked the complainant if he knew the boy, and he related that he had never seen him. I went to the back bedroom where the burglar had made prior entry into the home by breaking out the window and Lo! And Behold: the juvenile was inside the broken window, lifting a home stereo, getting ready to place it outside the window. I approached the juvenile. I asked: "having fun?" The juvenile turned and jumped me and I took him to the floor. In the meantime, I looked at the old man, and he was jumping up and down screaming: "what can I do Officer, what can I do". I very calmly told him "call the Police." (We didn't have portable radios in those days.) Before he could call, I had the kid in full custody.

Later, during the same patrol, I had another burglary call from Dispatch. Upon arrival at the home, the complaining party met me at the door to the home. He related that he had had a party the prior evening and when he woke up this morning, discovered that he had been burglarized and it must have been one of the partygoers.

I asked him, "What was missing?" He related: "A brick."

I asked: "What kind of brick?"

He responded: "You know, a Kilo." I asked: "A Kilo of what?"

At this point, he was starting to get upset with me. He motioned me to follow him to the kitchen. He opened the top freezer to his icebox saying, "I had four of them last night, now there are only three of them left."

He was pointing at three packaged Kilos of marijuana. He was not a bit understanding when I put handcuffs on him.

He kept insisting on a burglary report, all the way to jail.

# CURLY VII

One hot summer day while on Bicycle Patrol, my partner and I were southbound on Avenida Central. About 5 feet in front of us was this young couple in business attire. We could smell the Evil Weed. The couple was passing the Evil Weed back and forth after each took a hit. My partner pulled up beside the male just as he was taking it back from his girlfriend, reached over, and took the Evil Weed out of their hands. The male doubled up his fist, saying:

"You son of a bitch!"

The male then turned toward my partner, and upon seeing my partner said: "Oh Shit!"

Later that afternoon while riding along the Downtown Canal, I saw a Volkswagen Bug, floating and slowly drifting in the water. I rode along the canal and observed a man sitting in the drivers' seat. It was winter and I was not about to get wet; I decided to let the Fire Department save the man. Upon the Fire Department extracting the man from the vehicle, I asked him what happened.

He said: "This is not my day. I tried to cut my wrist and all it did was stop bleeding. Then I took a bunch of pills and all I did was vomit. So I drove off into the canal and I all did was float. This is not my day."

That night, several of us attended a "Choir Practice." I don't think anyone was under a .18 BAC (Blood Alcohol Count). Choir Practice is serious business!

During this particular event, we watched a 211 (Armed Robbery) go down across the street. The eight of us took the suspect into custody, handcuffed him to a pole, gave the store clerk the made-safe .25 Auto, and told him to call Crime Stop. Then the eight of us rode off into the sunrise.

Somehow the Officer in our Choir that used his handcuffs on the bad guy found them the next day at his station mailbox; no questions asked.

## CURLY VIII

Toward the end of a rather uneventful Shift on foot patrol, a lady came out of her apartment and told us the kids in the apartment above her had a rattlesnake in a cardboard box, next to her apartment. She pointed at the box. We thought she was just joking with us. We opened the lid on the box and sure as hell, there laid a two-foot Diamondback Rattlesnake. The funny part was the kids had been trying to feed the snake Cheerios, a nutritious breakfast cereal. The poor snake was skinny like it had not eaten in weeks, and it appeared to be half dead. How the kids were not bitten, I will never know.

Then there was the Fly problem. The Pendleton Projects Manager contacted us one day and asked us to go and talk to a lady who kept calling his office and complaining about flies. What flies have to do with enforcing the law, we couldn't figure out, but to keep the manager happy we walked to the lady's apartment.

Upon entering her apartment the smell was unbearable. We noticed that the ceiling had a wet spot and something was dripping from the apartment above hers. The ceiling is constructed of about a two-foot slab of concrete.

We obtained the apartment complex master key from the office. Upon opening the door to the upstairs apartment, there lay what was left of the decomposed body of an old lady.

The Medical Examiner reported that the deceased had expired of natural causes. That by itself was unusual enough for the Pendleton Projects.

*Chapter V*

# JAILS AND DETENTION

## INTRODUCTION:

In my home state, juvenile suspects upon arrest are detained in lockup facilities exclusively for persons aged eight to eighteen. These facilities are administered not by Police or Sheriff's Departments, but by Probation Departments. Juvenile detention facility staff consists of Probation Department employees, including a few Probation Officers who volunteer for a year or two of detention duty, for experience, and for "R and R." I did occasionally volunteer for detention duty. Why did I volunteer, and why did I enjoy my detention experiences? Read on.

# INSIDE

Inside, it is a different universe. Volumes have been written on this subject. More volumes could be written and undoubtedly will be. If you have never been an inmate of a jail or a prison for at least one year, or if you have not been a Detention or Corrections Officer for several years, it can be truly said that you don't know "Jack" about this subject. However, I hope that after reading this book, you will want to learn.

Whenever the subject of lockups and how they should be run comes up around me, it seems that people who have not experienced this life can't wait to tell me that they have all the definitive answers to all the questions regarding lockups and inmate behavior patterns and control. These answers will usually be based upon little if any personal experience. They will most likely be based upon information received from the entertainment media, academic types, pronouncements of politicians seeking reelection, or, worse, the news media.

As part of my career of more than thirty years, I worked inside the walls for more than ten years; during my final years, I trained new Detention Officers. Yet, as I write these words I find myself struggling for a way to paint with an accurate brush an easy-to-comprehend "Big Picture" of what life is like inside the Walls, Juvenile or Adult, for both inmates and staff.

It is Conventional Wisdom that most lockup inmates, male and female, resemble "Bubba;" that all inmates claim to be innocent, that all inmates want to get out, that life in the lockups is all violence. Well, life in a lockup certainly can be brutal, in a number of ways. It is true that for most people, living in a lockup would be frightening, but for more reasons than "Bubba's" presence. It is confining. In some such environments, noise and confusion abound; in others, the silence can be maddening. Life inside can be at times frightening, and at times, incredibly boring.

The inmates can be, at the same time, both intimidating and pathetic. And, although you and I may see life in a lockup as being second only to death, there are hundreds of thousands of prisoners who will do anything they need to do to ensure that they will not have to take responsibility for their lives and deal with the demands of the outside world. The release of those people who cannot, or will not, cope with life on the outside will often result in them setting themselves up for arrest as soon as possible after release from a lockup.

On the other side of the bars, there are thousands of wonderful, well-educated citizens employed as Officers inside detention facilities and prisons, working in environments most citizens don't wish to see, much less work in. These Officers typically take on their new responsibilities with unbelievably low starting wages. To me, it is a great source of frustration that these Officers are often so poorly trained and so poorly supported by their administrators that they typically quit in less than one year; far faster than they can be replaced.

Once again, in reality, life inside is not always one ongoing, 24-7, "Snake Pit." On occasion, good things do happen in jails and prisons, sometimes through the endeavors of detention staff, sometimes through the endeavors of inmates; sometimes both sides of the bars plan and work together for the common good. In particular, if an Officer can find ways to survive the stress of the job and somehow feed his family for a few years, experience and common sense developed by the Officer can result in a lot of wonderful things being done for and with inmates.

If you, as a citizen, wish to understand and/or deal with Detention and Corrections issues, you must first empty your head of preconceived notions handed to you over the years by the various "experts" who knew then less than you know now. Tour jails and prisons in your area. Converse with your Jail or Prison Tour guides and with their Agency Directors. Also, converse if you can with Line Officers who are doing the work inside.

In my opinion, the major problems within the field of Corrections become perpetuated as a result of public ignorance and/or indifference. Become informed, then if you agree with what I have written, speak up for improved conditions not only for inmates but also for Detention and Corrections Officers. Realize that inmates will for the most part be released one day, and will once again be residing in your neighborhood.

Many criminal activities that occur in the community are conceived of and planned inside the walls of Detention and Corrections facilities (Remember, I said life Inside can be boring at times; what do you suppose inmates think about when they're bored?). With more, well-trained Officers and with more truly realistic programs within the walls we could make some positive strides with more inmates.

## SOME MAJOR DIFFERENCES

To review, prisons are usually owned and operated by a State Department of Corrections. Inmates are convicted felons (very serious crimes) who will serve at least one year inside. Jails and detention facilities are usually owned and operated by counties and cities. These facilities generally house two types of inmates: persons sentenced on misdemeanor convictions (less serious crimes) who will max out in one year or less, and persons who are awaiting Court action and who may not yet have been found guilty of anything.

With the exception of issues requiring maximum confinement in either kind of facility, jails are most often more restrictive, in terms of prisoner movement and activity, than are prisons. This is true for numerous very good reasons, which are not necessary to enter into at this point. In general, "Cons" will tell you they are more comfortable in prison than in jail, primarily because they do have more freedoms.

I know I am about to deeply traumatize the tender psyches of any number of Sheriffs who like to loudly proclaim in their reelection campaigns that they do not tolerate any guff from the Felons residing inside their Jails. In reality, Sheriffs' Jails routinely house few, if indeed, any, convicted Felons. Felons are most often residing in a

State Prison. Sheriffs operate County Jails. For the most part, Persons who reside in Jails are those who have been convicted of Misdemeanors, and also those who have not yet been convicted of anything, or have been convicted and now are awaiting a Sentencing Hearing; in any case, they are awaiting further Court activity. I often wish that some of the "Tough" would apply more energy toward Staff trainin and development of more effective programs than toward building public relations monuments for themselves.

During recent years there has been a major movement toward privatizing prisons and jails. There are a number of reasons why politicians justify this movement, mostly economic. As a retired officer and now a private citizen I will say I have not one favorable opinion to offer regarding privately owned and operated jails and prisons. My reasons will become clear as this book progresses.

Anyway, whether I like it or not, private jails and prisons do exist in the United States. How they are operated will vary, depending upon the policies of their Parent Company State and Federal laws, the expressed needs of the contracting government entities, and, primarily, of course, economics. Within the walls, the education and experiential backgrounds of the staff will vary, depending upon the employee entry-level, the qualifications set by the Parent Company and policies, and the preferences of the Wardens in charge. The staff training curriculum and schedules, as well as salaries, will vary as well.

Before I go any further, I acknowledge that I have been hammering on the issue of staff training. I am a fanatic on this issue because I believe that in any kind of organization, without appropriate and adequate pre-service and ongoing in-service training, there will be no success for the organization or the employee.

Research the number of Officer-inmate verbal and physical combats occurring within your local jail or prison. In some lockups, the injuries and deaths resulting from such confrontations result in millions of dollars of tax money expended in lawsuits, mostly settled out of court. What I want you to think about is this: the majority of these confrontations begin with words. Words result in blows. Blows usually degenerate into grappling and going to the floor. This means that there will likely be injuries. It has been my experience that during most of these confrontations, as a consequence of inadequate training, the staff themselves unwittingly accelerated these incidents into violent endings.

## WHY DOES ANYONE WANT TO WORK THERE?

Well, in my case, I saw volunteering for a year or two of duty in a Juvenile Detention Facility as a chance for a little "R and R." It is one of the oddities of the Criminal Justice System that while in most cases Sheriffs and Police Chiefs operate County and City jails, those Probation Department Chiefs responsible for the supervision of juvenile offenders are also usually responsible for County-level Juvenile Detention Facilities as well. Often this oddity affords Probation staff opportunities to serve in various positions within the Juvenile Detention Facility for a time. It is not unusual in some communities for Juvenile Probation Officers to begin their careers as Detention Officers. What an excellent way for a total Rookie in the Justice System to be exposed to all sides of adolescent behavior!

Here in Cordova City, the Adult and Juvenile Probation Departments have the same Chief. Duty assignments within the Adult Department or the Juvenile Divisions, both Probation and Detention, were assigned by the Chief to Officers he believed best suited. Within the Juvenile Departments, a Probation Officer could request an assignment to work with juveniles in the Detention Facility. Therefore, upon my request, one fine day I was awarded a transfer to the Juvenile Detention Facility. There not being at the time formal training for working in Juvenile Detention as well as for working Probation Caseloads, when I entered Detention, I was trained on the job: "Here's your key."

I began my new assignment in the cellblock for juveniles who were awaiting a Judicial Decision regarding whether they would be adjudicated as juveniles or as adults. This decision would profoundly affect their lives. In most States, a Juvenile Court Judge has the power to order any juvenile over eight years of age to be tried as an adult. Yes, under certain conditions, I mean ANY juvenile over eight years of age! Remember the twelve-year-old boy I wrote of in a prior chapter? The young men in my assigned cellblock were awaiting this very decision regarding their cases.

These young men usually took their plight very seriously, and therefore they were very worried as to what the Court might do with them. Consequently, as a general rule, this cellblock tended to be free of serious behavioral problems, at least from the inmates. This environment is largely trouble-free in terms of inmate behavior, it was a great place for me to begin what promised to be at least two years of Detention duty.

# ROACHES AND CRICKETS

By the time I began engaging in casework within the Juvenile Detention facility, the ancient Detention Facility I'd written of in Chapter One was long gone. The Juvenile Detention Division by now boasted a total of three new facilities, each with a capacity of 300 persons under the age of eighteen years. This expansion was a consequence of the State's rapid growth in population. Our County's Adult Detention Facilities at this time had expanded to five separate Jails.

Just a quick aside: the County Jail maintained exclusively for women is situated across a small field from the County's Mens' Minimum Security Facility. Until security procedures were stepped up in this location, some male inmates would depart from their Minimum

Facility at night, during "Lights Out," to sneak over to the Women's

The facility to peek into the women's windows. Ah, These small delights in life . . .

As one would expect, roaches and crickets abound within institutional facilities such as jails and prisons. Roaches were invented to be Nature's Little Scavengers of organic refuse. On the Economic side of life, roaches also help promote the careers of pest control professionals. So, can anyone tell me why were crickets invented?

Crickets are ubiquitous, noisy, nasty, clothes-eating bugs. Pest exterminators contracted by the County make regular visits to all our Adult and Juvenile Facilities, to little avail.

Crickets occasionally provide entertainment inside the lockups. Shades of Robert Stroud, "The Birdman of Alcatraz," a few ingenious inmates will find ways to hook the little guys up to micro-sized carts and sleds made of paper. Inmates, much to the delight of all, including the Officers, sometimes stage cricket races. Some occasional inmates attempt to draw attention to themselves by publicly biting off the heads of the hapless little crickets. Today, of course, on a "Grossness Scale," television's "Reality" shows far outstrip such inmate behavior.

Roaches, on the other hand, were at the time of my service in the Detention Division a rarity, at least within the Juvenile facilities. This was a result of good general hygiene on the part of Staff and Inmates as well as visits by our contracted extermination professionals. I like to believe that an incident I took part in helped to promote our roach-free environment, as well as possibly cause a little Administrative heartburn over at the Sheriff's Main Jail.

For reasons that I hope are obvious, Detention Officers and Probation Officers engaged in casework within the Detention Facility accompany and supervise inmates at the eating area during meal times. The rewards for staff doing this include the bliss of enjoying ongoing security, and, if desired, a free meal, such as it may be. Many knowledgeable staff will instead send out for pizza, Chinese, Mega-Wonder-Burgers; anything not put together by the jail or prison food preparation system. The reason for this is clear: inmates prepare the food.

On one particular afternoon, I accompanied a group of young men, mostly seventeen years of age, to the afternoon meal in one of the Juvenile Detention Facilities in Cordova City. The Cuisine Du Jour was spaghetti and meat sauce. While preparing to enjoy his meal, one of the inmates, an African- American youth named Billy Burke called across his table for my attention.

"Hey, Nee Man, c'mere a look at this!" "What, Billy?" "Well, c'mere!"

I walked to Billy's table. I saw the objects of Billy's complaint regarding his plate of food: there were roaches mixed into his meat sauce.

Billy said, "Well, Nee Man, watchoo gonna do bout this?"

I said, "Billy, I think you ought to write a letter about this to the Judge."

Silly me. Billy did write a letter to the Presiding Juvenile Court Judge. After the Presiding Judge read Billy's letter, His Honor sent a copy of Billy's letter to me, along with a Direct Order that I investigate how roaches came to be included in Billy's spaghetti and meat sauce.

I read Billy's letter to the Presiding Judge. Billy's letter was carefully printed. What follows is Billy's letter:

> This is ~~[redacted]~~ 4/11/79
>
> Dear Sir. 1:05
> I was eating in the Cafitea
> and I come up on a roach.
> Then I sit there Five secon.
> and one of my Frined said Take
> it up There and show him. Shit.
> My Frined is Ricky.F. I give my plate
> To John.off and He give it to L.m White.
> and Sir. This is my Frined AlBiert.L. Talken
> ow. Sir. This iain't The First Time we
> Found roaches in are Food.
> We have Found roaches in are punch.
> I know This ain't know Hotel.
> But we Should have a decent meal.
> Will sir. I hope you put a stop
> To This. and again Sir. This ain't know
> Hotel, but I think the reason
> My Stonach is hurting me
> cuz I have Eating to
> my roaches.
> I would write Botter But
> my stomack hurt.
> Sincerely. ~~[redacted]~~
>
> RECEIVED
> APR 10 1979
> JUDGE T.
> SUPERIOR
>
> I Think you

I did see roaches in Billy's food. It was the last day I have ever drawn an Institutional meal.

My investigation revealed that the County employed six paid kitchen staff, including two cooks, at the main Adult Jail. This staff supervised thirty prisoners, who prepared, cooked, and packaged all the food for transport to all the County's lockups. The six paid staff supervised these prisoners from inside a glass-walled office, which was raised and overlooking the Jail kitchen area.

During my investigation, I discovered a number of issues and behaviors, which interfered with inmates receiving healthy and non-contaminated food.

The most important issues were these:

Non-kitchen Detention staff and various contract workers from outside, e.g., pest exterminators and food suppliers, were a disruption to both sanitation and work routine.

Caught on videotape were inmates assigned to kitchen duty tossing into food vats, and trays of food: roaches, cigarettes, parts of shoes and underwear, and other, sometimes really bizarre, items. During my investigation, one inmate was arrested and charged for urinating into a vat of punch.

Prisoners on kitchen duty told me the County kitchen employees rarely left their glass-walled office to interact or interfere with inmate behavior because the Supervisors were afraid of the inmates.

I was told several months after I filed my investigation report that the paid County staff at the time of the investigation were all terminated and replaced.

## BITE ME

During a physical altercation in one of our Juvenile Detention Facilities between Detention staff and three inmates in a "holding tank" containing forty-five inmates, I received a bite from an inmate on my left arm. At the time that I responded to Detention Central Communication's "All Available Staff" alarm, a "Dog Pile," that is, as many hyper-excited Officers as possible, mindlessly but enthusiastically piled on top of an unknown number of inmates, was already in effect.

I hated to see the "Dog Pile;" however, this kind of staff reaction to the physical crisis is ubiquitous in institutional settings. I entered into the fray, and during the resolution of this crisis, I did fail to exercise as much caution as I should have. Consequently, I did receive a bite.

Biting and spitting happens a lot during physical altercations in institutional settings. Special anti-biting/anti spitting equipment, such as hoods, can be purchased from reputable institutional supply organizations. While I was "Fearless Leader" of the Juvenile Detention Officer Academy, we received a shipment of "spit hoods;" a hood which, when called for, is secured over the out-of-control inmate's head so that the inmate's opportunity to spit becomes nonexistent. The hood, being constructed of a combination of solid fabric, with closely woven netting for the inmate's eyes, the inmate's vision will also be severely curtailed. I brought a "spit hood" into a Supervisors' meeting one day, with an intent to make known the availability to Detention staff of these items, and in order to brief Shift Supervisors on the proper application of the hoods. A Detention Sergeant took one of the hoods, carefully pulled it over her head, moved her head around a little, then complained: "We can't use these; the staff won't be able to see a damned thing wearing them!" God's Truth, that's exactly what she said.

I will wager a chunk of my State Pension that rare indeed is the Criminal Justice Agency that is politically and economically ready to spend sufficient funds for all the quality, ongoing, training needed to assure that Detention Facilities would be safe and up to date and that Staff training will be up to date as well. In all fairness, at the same time, I sense that Criminal Justice, or the Government for that matter, is not alone in this sad fact.

It both astounds and saddens me when I research the amount of funds lost by Government agencies through settled litigation. How much of this could have been prevented by allocating more on Staff Development, rather than on settlement of lawsuits?

The responsibility for all this should not rest entirely upon the heads of Department Chiefs. As I have examined, and in some cases, experienced, a number of nationally marketed organizations offering crisis prevention or intervention training programs, it is my opinion that none offer truly viable verbal and physical intervention techniques, at least not for Staff working in the Criminal Justice System's institutional facilities. Yet Detention Facility Chiefs, I believe not knowing any better, tend to buy into these "One-Size-Fits-All", one-weekend-per-year, "crisis resolution" programs, and either believe or hope that this "training" is all that's needed to keep everyone safe.

And, yes, I AM an expert on this subject, and some of my written efforts in this area have included Students and Instructors' training manuals, addressing crisis prevention and verbal and physical techniques designed to minimize the chances of injury. Note the word: "minimize;" no training program can guarantee an injury-free incident.

The major problem one encounters in a crisis is called "Primary Default." Persons trained in understanding and dealing with this concept can help to save the day. Ignorance of this concept can result in disaster. The concept of "Primary Default" is simply this: in a crisis, any person involved will react to the crisis in a manner reflecting his/her most recent level of training, or lack thereof.

A void in training can invite injury, death, and, you can be certain, litigation. Without proper training, Staff responding to a melee will most likely lead with emotions and, of course, with adrenaline. So it was when I entered the aforementioned cellblock on that fine April afternoon. Three inmates and eighteen officers were rolling about on the cellblock floor; all were shouting, swearing, swinging, and kicking! As a minimum goal, I decided to work on assisting the Officers involved regain self-control. I did not pay attention as closely as I always demand of my Academy and my martial arts students, and as a result, I received a bite.

Once the incident was brought to near-total calm and it was time for report writing, the Detention Chief told me to check out of the Detention Facility and proceed to an outfit called "Urgent Care" for treatment for the bite on my arm. I did depart, mounted my motorcycle, and drove to "Urgent Care." Upon my arrival, I discovered that "Urgent Care" was closed for the weekend. How poetic. I then contacted a friend who is a Fire Department paramedic. Problem solved. Then, we then celebrated my somewhat less-than-heroic heroic behavior with a bit of scotch. Now, that is what I call excellent "urgent care!"

## WHERE'D HE GO? WHERE'D HE GO?

In my opinion, a major portion of any viable crisis resolution training program must be dedicated toward helping people to find ways to remain calm and focused, from the first misguided or hostile word, regardless of who speaks it, or the first attempted strike or grab, regardless of who attempts it, to the final gasps of the incident, including the final surges of adrenaline.

Losing visual contact with a belligerent person can be an embarrassment. On an evening following dinnertime in our Main Juvenile Detention Facility, an outburst occurred between two very large seventeen-year-old inmates. An alarm was sounded and the facility's P.A. system cried for "All Available Staff."

I responded to the call, as did a dozen other Officers. When we appeared on the scene, there was the "Dog Pile." It was large, and it was positioned in the center of the Cell Block day room. The only sounds I heard when I entered the Cell Block was those of heavily breathing Officers. Along the walls of the day, the room stood inmates and a few Officers who had taken the responsibility of attending to those non-combating inmates.

The Shift Sergeant appeared. He directed that staff piled on top of each other on the center of the floor rise and that the combatants be secured and transported to their cells.

The Officers involved in the "Dog Pile" arose and stood. Hark: there were no inmates on the bottom of the Pile! The "out-of-control" inmates were found to be standing along the wall, along with all the other inmates, observing the action on the center of the floor.

On another occasion, the outcome was a little different.

When I arrived on the scene of that particular "Dog Pile," one of the two combatants at the time was standing, well secured by two Detention Officers, a safe distance away.

An Officer participating in the "Dog Pile" asked the youth on the bottom:

"Are you okay now?"

The young man underneath replied: "Yeah."

Upon hearing "Yeah," ALL the involved Officers stood up and backed away from the unsecured, still angry youth. The young inmate jumped up, charged at the other, secured, former combatant, and pummeled him while the two attending Officers momentarily stood there, slack-jawed, and watched.

# NOT ALL GLOOM AND DOOM

Despite all that I have written, not all live in a lockup is invariably gloom and doom. Good things can happen when promising prospective Officers are hired, well trained, and encouraged by their Supervisors to be more than just stern, uniformed, maximum-security Prison Guards. I experienced the pleasures of working with quite a few really fine Officers while I was assigned to duty inside the Walls. Not all these fine Officers Were Probation Officers taking up temporary positions, enjoying some much-deserved "R and R" in Detention. Many were hired specifically as Detention Officers, some of whom were aspiring to eventually qualify to become Probation Officers; others preferred to remain working as Detention Officers permanently.

It has long been my opinion that possessing a College or University Degree in Social Work, Criminal Justice, Public Administration or Psychology should not necessarily be a mandatory requisite for working with offenders, Adult or Juvenile. In my opinion, the primary requisite needs to be: a well-centered person who has no need or desire to present as anyone other than himself or herself. In other words, in my opinion, good, effective Officers are born, not made. Yes, I am aware that in some professional circles this will be seen as heresy.

My favorite and I believe most positively productive, co-workers, were persons who tended to be far from the vanilla mold. Clearly, Curly and I are not of that mold. Nor, I am happy to state, is the person who took over the

Detention Officers academy when I retired. That Officer was with me from the time I wrote the first word in the first Detention Officers Manual.

Another, truly colorful partner was a Latina colleague in Juvenile Detention I called, by way of affection, "The Mamacita." As off-the-wall as some of her ideas and behavior could appear to be at times, when the ca-ca hit the fan, The Mamacita could be relied upon to maintain her focus and establish control over very bad situations. She also conducted a number of great programs with detained kids.

Good Officers know when to be relatively relaxed, when to be firm, and when to call for an Officer-inmate group discussion regarding issues needing immediate resolution. Sometimes, producing something positive means being a bit more creative than is usually expected; that is, "thinking outside the box" (No pun intended.) Our Detention Officers have produced talent shows, sometimes featuring both inmates and Officers. Concerts and plays from colleges and some very generous professional performers have found a way inside to provide entertainment. G.E.D. classes and Twelve-step programs are not uncommon. To the best of my knowledge, not one Officer or inmate has been killed or injured as a result of any of these events.

The Officers who create these kinds of programs know that the inmates are going to be outside the Walls one day. These Officers are trying to find ways to help inmates decide to change their behavior so that they don't come back. And some former prisoners do not come back.

# WARRIORS IN JUVENILE DETENTION

During the period that I opened a T'ai Chi program for juveniles in the County Juvenile Detention Facilities, I was serving another Detention duty. At that time, I noted that over the years little in the way of daily Detention routine had changed: regular Detention staff had had little to no pre-service training many Detention Officers staff had some great ideas, but no real understanding of juvenile behavior (for example, what constitutes "normal" adolescent or juvenile behavior, as opposed to what would constitute "criminal" behavior), or of incident prevention or intervention techniques.

Juveniles in Detention still enjoyed obtaining Officer attention, in whatever way possible. When a crisis occurred, Detention staff generally overreacted, and again, in my opinion, Administrators failed to adequately train personnel in prevention or intervention techniques. So, which group: college-educated staff, or troubled juveniles, seemed more likely to be willing to learn self-discipline and alternatives to physical over-reaction?

Well, perhaps the reader may have heard of an ancient Zen parable, entitled "A Cup Of Tea," wherein the Master fills a visitor's cup to overflow, and when the visitor protests, the Master says: "Like this cup, you are full of your own opinions. How can I teach you unless you first empty your cup?"

In our Detention Facility, The staff's "cups" were mostly full; the juveniles' "cups" were mostly empty. Therefore: enter the Tai Chi Program For Detained

Children. From the beginning of the T'ai Chi program, approved (with some trepidations) by the Chief Probation Officer, the reactions in Detention were, for the most part: enthusiasm from the juveniles and fear and uproar from the staff ("my God, he's teaching kids how to attack staff!"). Of course, I offered the same T'ai Chi program to Detention Officers: twelve Officers (out of 200) showed interest and trained with me. Two of the twelve Officers with me were Willie, who would one day Head up the Juvenile Detention Academy and The Mamacita.

The Tai Chi classes for detained juveniles generally consisted of eight to thirty students in each class. There were two classes daily, five days per week. Of course, there was a "Belt" program; advancement through white, yellow, orange, and blue belts promoted self-respect in the student and a desire to achieve further. The juveniles were proud of this physical evidence of achievement, and in the two years of the programs existence, not one of my students exhibited a behavior problem in Detention. Even the white (beginner) belt had to be earned: "prospects" would read Master Peter Hill's <u>G.E.T. IT. TOGETHER,</u> a wonderful book is written for persons attempting to "find" themselves and excel in their lives. They were orally tested on the book's content and also demonstrate at least minimal competence in "The Eight Essentials," as well as basic stances and movements used in the practices of T'ai Chi and Chi Gung.

Six months into the program, detained juveniles with "colored belts" were participating in the training of detained juveniles wearing white belts.

Testing procedures for belts and award ceremonies were duly elaborate.

At last, the T'ai Chi program achieved credibility: the students were being invited to perform demonstrations, by teachers, Judges, and Juvenile Probation Administrators.

Eventually, a greater number of Detention Officers noted and became interested in the program. When the Juvenile Detention Officers Academy opened, T'ai Chi was integrated into the program.

Now, some twelve years later, I still on occasion hear stories of some of my former Detention students who have found better lives for themselves: real jobs, high school completions; some went through college (one is now a practicing attorney; should this be counted as a "success?" Hmmm!). Some even continued in the Martial Arts.

My goal was for students to have a solid knowledge of their strengths, their weaknesses, and how to be in control of themselves by the time they earned the orange belt. Knowing who you are---and who you are not, is a critically important concept for self-development. Accepting yourself, to make all things better for yourself and your loved ones is a good start toward "rehabilitation."

# HEAD UP AND LOCKED UP

How many well-intentioned people have I watched enter into the field of Criminal Justice, particularly in the Juvenile arena, who truly believed that "If you just show them a little love..." That's a very nice concept; however, there's a lot more to this game than "Love one another" on both sides of the Badge.

Enter, for example, Probation Officer George Womack. George was a holder of a Master's Degree in Social Work, and a former Children's Services Caseworker from New York City. George made it clear to me when he participated in my Juvenile Detention Officers Academy that he had left Children's Services and joined us so that he would be in possession of more legal power, to be able to better affect the lives of persons he touched in the System.

I have known many M.S.W.'s who have set themselves up in the business of providing family therapy. Some have been very effective. Some have done far better work, in my opinion, than several Ph.D.'s I have known. However, this was not to be necessarily true of Officer George Womack. While a Field Probation Officer, parents and juveniles alike had threatened George; he was punched on two occasions by parents (yes, the parents were prosecuted), and, allegedly, shot at once. The Chief wisely placed George in an environment where he hopefully would be safer: a Juvenile Detention Facility.

George was assigned to the cellblock housing the "Little Guys," juveniles aged eight to twelve years. George "related" to the Little Guys right away. George loved to play with the Little Guys. Occasionally, a co-worker would complain that George got so involved with the children that he had his "head up and locked;" in other words, it appeared that George was oblivious to the behavior of those other children in the Cellblock not engaged with him in play at any given time. I have no idea as to how George responded to his Supervisor regarding all this. After completing the Detention Officers Academy, George was no longer my responsibility, Deo Gracias.

On one day in particular, during his shift, George was assigned to remain on the cellblock assigned to the Little Guys, while his partner took their charges to the meal area for lunch. One Officer needed to remain behind because a seventeen-year-old solitary confined inmate was locked up in one of the cells there in the Little Guys' Cellblock. The seventeen-year-old confined inmate's endless shouting, screaming and door banging had eventually worn out all the Officers in all the other cellblocks, as well as the respective juvenile inmates; now he was confined in the last unscathed cellblock, the one for the Little Guys.

According to the Incident Report written later regarding the incident that day involving George and this confined inmate, the pounding and screaming emanating from the inmate's cell began to disturb George. George therefore, decided to exercise his considerable negotiating skills with the inmate.

George walked to the inmate's cell and entered into conversation with the inmate with a goal toward peace negotiation: that is, giving the inmate something in exchange for some prolonged, blessed, silence. The inmate told George that he wanted to telephone his mother. The inmate represented to George that, if only he could make this call, his mother would drive to our Detention Facility and, somehow, remove her son from us bad Detention guys.

George explained to the inmate that providing a confined person with a telephone call to Mother was not possible. Sorry!

George returned to the cellblock office. Immediately George was treated to Pound! Pound! Scream! Pound! Pound! Scream!

Once again, George loudly proclaimed his demand for Silence!

The response: Pound! Pound! Scream! Pound! Pound! Scream!

At length, George asked the inmate to promise, Honest-To-God, that if he were allowed to call his mother, supervised, of course, by George, that there would be total, blessed eternal silence thereafter. The inmate promised.

George unlocked and opened the cell door. The inmate grabbed George and threw him across the cell, onto the cell bed. The confinee closed the cell door and locked it, with George inside.

At this time the door pounding resumed; however, George was doing the pounding. The inmate was using the telephone to call his Mother.

When George's partner arrived at the Cellblock with the Little Guys, it was to the tune of door pounding, and the marvelous sight of the seventeen-year-old inmate, sitting in the staff office chair, feet resting on the staff desk, telephone in hand, speaking with his mother.

George's partner duly sounded the "All Available Staff" alarm.

An hour later, a very confused lady, claiming to be the mother of our confined inmate, appeared at the Main Door to our Detention Facility, wondering why her son was not ready to go home with her.

## I'VE GOT A SECRET

At least once weekly, and if deemed necessary, sometimes more often, total "strip searches" are made of all the cellblocks in all Adult and Juvenile Detention Facilities. For obvious reasons there are no set, or scheduled, days or times for searches conducted of each cellblock; they occurred as randomly as possible, however, strip searches of each cellblock did need to occur at least once weekly.

Inmates' hiding places for contraband can be ingenious. Only if you've worked in an institutional setting can you begin to imagine how inventive? and devious these "dumb crooks" can be! At the same time, sometimes the seemingly "smartest" inmates can do some dumb things.

During a search of the Young Women's "First Offender" Cellblock ("first Offender" in this case really means "The first time in Detention"), an Officer located a rolled-up clear plastic bag, containing what appeared to be the classic "Green Leafy Substance." The cylinder-shaped object was approximately ten inches long and was a bit over one inch in diameter. The object had a strong, pungent odor, not at all resembling the odor of what would be the suspected marijuana within.

The object found during the search was located under a female inmate's pillow.

The Shift Supervisor was called. As was called for, an Incident Report was written and Police were notified. The object in question was bagged and tagged and transported by Cordova City Police Officers to their crime lab.

The young female inmate from whose bed the object was confiscated, no surprise, had no idea the object had been there, had no idea what the object was, had never seen the object, had no idea how the object came to be in her cell in the first place.

Two days later, the crime lab results returned: Marijuana inside the baggie, a human fecal matter outside the baggie. Yes, this young "First Offender" had entered our Detention Facility with the pot "Keester Stashed." (For the Uninitiated, that means "Rectally Inserted.") Later, she confessed that she'd been smoking once per night, while lying in her Detention bed, since she'd been jailed, two weeks earlier. Until the fateful day of discovery, she'd been keeping her stash anally secured, expelling it whenever she wished to smoke, then reinserting the bag until next time. On this particular day, she'd fallen asleep without re-stashing her stash. She stated that she did recall her error during a class in the Detention School. Too late: at that time, the fateful strip search was being conducted!

Training Note: This is one of many examples as to why surgical gloves must be worn while conducting any search.

# A QUOTE TO PONDER

Every time I've heard it, it has made my jaws clench. It is most often said by people who have absolutely no emotional attachment to anyone or anything, usually not even to himself or herself. It is easy to dismiss these people as "Sociopathic Personalities," "losers," "pond scum." It is not so easy to deal with them when damages to victims must be addressed, and when there can be no doubt that there will be further victims in the future.

The young offender was returned to our Detention Facility by the Detention Transportation staff. He had just made a Court appearance. At that appearance, a plea negotiation was entered into, whereby the offender admitted to "Attempted Auto Theft." Five other felony Auto Theft charges were dismissed. These "Plea Negotiations," it is said, are necessary in order to accelerate cases through the heavily calendared Courts. The values or lack thereof in the plea negotiation process have been discussed for decades.

I was asked to search the young man for re-entry into Detention. He was visibly agitated; fortunately, he knew me and decided to not cause trouble. I began to enter into small talk, a tool frequently used to calm new arrivals, or at least (hopefully) to prevent violent outbursts.

The conversation went like this:

"Hey Felix, you back from Court?" "Yeah."

"The Judge says that you gonna stay with us?" "Yeah"

"When's your next Court?" "March sixteen."

"What's gonna happen?"

"Man, shouldn't nothing happen." "Whaddya mean?"
"I dint do nothing to nobody."

"Felix, didn't you steal cars?" "Yeah. So what?"

"So, stealing somebody's car doesn't hurt them?"

"Hell, no, man! They got insurance!"

So, that's it. If you are insured, you can't be hurt. Right?

# ANOTHER QUOTE

Have you ever seen advertised, or attended, one of those all-day, often Police Department-sponsored, "One-Size-Fits-All" ladies self-defense classes?

Yes, I know, sometimes martial arts schools will also offer this type of workshop. I have offered and taught dozens of ladies' self-defense classes. The women's self-defense classes my "G.E.T. I.T. TOGETHER™" Schools' martial arts colleagues and I teach, however, are generally a total of six half-days in length and include manuals and, at times, actual full-contact sparring. "Too rough for women," you say? Fine. As an alternative, all you need to do is to ensure that for all the world's men, women, and children in the future, armed robbers will work more softly on their victims.

Ladies, has anyone told you that if an attacker grabs at you, you should scream or blow a whistle? This, you have been assured, will unnerve your attacker, and most likely he will flee right away. In any event, help is sure to be on the way, your scream having certainly been heard by a multitude of others, all of whom will be now running to your aid.

For example, just like the good citizens of New York City failed to rush to the aid of one Ms. Kitty Genovese, at the time when she was attacked and then stabbed to her death, in broad daylight, in front of her apartment, before dozens of onlookers.

I had a rare opportunity to discuss this very kind of situation with a fourteen-year-old male inmate at the Eastside branch of Juvenile Detention. He had been the perpetrator of an armed robbery gone badly. He had been armed with a handgun at the time.

During an early December evening on the East side of Cordova City, fourteen-year-old Derek Abel positioned himself outside a large chain grocery store. He was looking for any lady with a large purse, hopefully full of cash. He had run two days before from his most recent foster home. The money he had stolen from that household was long gone. He was hungry. He was in no mood to return to Children's Services.

At last, a likely prospect appeared. The targeted lady exited the market with two grocery carts and a large purse. Derek followed the lady to her car.

Once there, he grabbed for the lady's purse. The lady screamed!

Derek shot her dead. He emptied the entire magazine of the handgun--- fifteen rounds---into her body. He grabbed the lady's purse and ran.

Derek was arrested less than one week following this robbery-homicide. The prosecutor successfully maneuvered Derek into the Adult Criminal Courts. Within ninety days of his arrest, Derek was charged, tried, convicted, and sentenced to twenty-five years to life.

As I helped him pack his gear and ready him for his ride to state prison aboard a Sheriff's bus, I took the opportunity to ask him:

"Derek, why did you shoot her?"

His response: "Man, her screaming pissed me off!"

# A PRIVATE PRISON STORY

Imagine yourself to be a prisoner. Your home State, for economic reasons, has contracted to send you and hundreds of your fellow inmates to a prison in a different State. You have now become a resident of that out-of-State prison. Sometime after establishing residence in your new prison, you and others in your cellblock become subjects in a videotape, created by that prison's Officers.

This videotape shows you and other inmates being bitten by Prison Officers' dogs and being prodded by Officers with stun guns. You are being forced to crawl, naked, while being kicked and beaten by Officers' batons.

The Prison Administration was allegedly using this videotape, according to subsequent FBI investigation reports, for training purposes.

The subsequent newspaper headline reporting this FBI Investigation can be found on page 3-A, USA Today, the Wednesday, August 20, 1997 issue. It reads, in part:

"On Video: Inmates Bitten, Beaten."

"FBI looking into possible rights violations."

At issue were practices being investigated in a particular privately operated prison, located in Texas. That's Texas, USA, 1997, not Auschwitz, Poland; 1945. One of their prisoners could be your friend, your neighbor, your relative, or yourself. One day these prisoners will be once again out on your streets and in your neighborhoods. Is this behavior on the part of prison staff going to make you safer?

*Chapter VI*

# "HOMES" AWAY FROM HOME

## INTRODUCTION:

Occasionally, the courts will order placement of a juvenile or an adult in a "Foster Setting." This sort of action can be for a laundry list of reasons; most often it is done because the court believes intensive treatment, including removal from the immediate community, is needed, but incarceration in a lockup facility is not.

This chapter will explore the operation of a number of the residential treatment facilities I dealt with as a Probation Officer, and the experiences of my clients living in them.

# WHAT KIND OF "HOMES?"

What kind of "home," and legal issues around "Placement" in a "home," depends upon the nature of the "home" and the nature of the "resident." Residential Treatment Facilities, or "RTC's," exist for so many different types of persons in need of services. There are Residential Treatment Facilities for the very young and for the very old; for innumerable various disabilities, including some disabilities recognized for centuries, some newly recognized, some yet to be recognized (or invented); for juvenile and adult criminal offenders; for persons with addictive personalities of the various stripe; for abused children; for abused adults. There are in addition, of course, detention and corrections facilities, "halfway houses" and "retreats." There are even more categories; however, by this time I hope you get the general idea of the scope of this subject.

There are National and Local Laws relating to, and regulating, each type of Residential Program. State and local agencies exist to license and oversee them. Sometimes the nature of the home and its services and its residents will result in licensing and supervision by several different National, State, and Local authorities. In these cases, the Directors and the Staff of these "homes" will often be required to operate by rules ranging from vague, to confusing to conflicting.

My experience over the years in doing business with privately owned and operated residential programs has caused me to be of the opinion that if you have a loved one residing in any program of any kind, your loved one is best served by your diligence, not just the Governments', in supervising that program and its administration, staff, and supervisors. I have seen Residential Programs Wonderful and Residential Programs Horrible. Most that I have done business with have performed at least acceptably for the persons I have supervised in my capacity as a Probation Officer. When we had offenders, adults, and juvenile, in "halfway houses," foster homes, or group homes, the Probation Officer was responsible to the Court as reporters on the progress of the Probationer and the viability of the Residential Program.

The length of residence for a "client" in any program will be a function partially of the progress, or lack thereof, of the resident, and partially, often most, of economics. There have been occasions when I have been frustrated to the hilt with some programs that I have needed to deal with, wherein "When "the insurance runs out, you're 'cured.'" In my State, it is the norm for a Juvenile Residential Treatment Center to charge an average $5000.00 per month, per juvenile. Because it is usually seen that this would be a stiff monthly bill for most families to meet, that $5000.00 per month, per juvenile, the bill is usually paid with taxpayers' money.

# GIMME BACK, MY KID!

Remember the family "drama triangle?"
Residential Treatment Programs often work with not only the Resident but also others who are significant in the

Resident's life. From a therapeutic perspective, that can be both a wonderful and an incredibly difficult challenge. Recall all the devious and bizarre behaviors I've described in this book so far (not mine, I mean the Probationers and their families!).

Understand that I'm describing only the experiences I've personally experienced in some way or another. Multiply that by two hundred million or so. Then imagine yourself as a Therapist, responsible for the treatment of thirty or so of these families at any one time, all having their agenda.

Here is a typical history: Don and Barbara have three children. Nat, fourteen, is the oldest. Nat is beginning to feel the testosterone level rising within his body, and he's having a tough time dealing with mood swings. Barbara is having problems with mood swings as well: she is going through menopause. The two younger children, both girls, are spoiled little "Princesses," who are beginning to act out in protest to all the attention Nat's increasingly rebellious behavior is garnering from Don and Barbara.

Don is working harder and later, or, at least, so he's telling Barbara, all the time. This is putting more pressure on Barbara to deal with the children, while, at the same time, she is trying to deal with herself; all this, with less and less support from Don.

One evening, Nat is arrested for auto theft. Now the Juvenile Court is making certain demands on Don and Barbara as well as Nat. Neither parent feels as though the other is supportive; both wish Nat would just "straighten up and fly right." They decide that now that Nat is on probation, it is the Probation Officer's job, not theirs, to "fix" Nat. Accordingly, the assigned P.O. decides that family counseling is called for.

Don and Barbara view the Court Order for family counseling as the State is blaming them for Nat's misdeeds. Therefore, during the time they attend the first two sessions with the Therapist, they bitterly blame the Police, the Court, and, especially, the P.O., as well as the schools for their plight. Soon afterward, they begin to miss appointments. At home, no night is allowed to pass without parents loudly blaming each other, and, of course, Nat, for all the family turmoil. Nat usually screams: "Fuck off!" and retreats to his room. He then slams his door and punches a few more holes in the drywall in his bedroom.

Soon enough, Nat steals another car. In Court, Don and Barbara tell the Judge: had the Probation Officer done his job, Nat would not have been in trouble again. But because the P.O. is NOT doing his job, the entire family is in constant uproar, and now they want the Court to place Nat "In a Home," at least until he has his head on straight.

The Court then decides to place Nat at the "Sunny Horizons Boys Ranch." Now, Don and Barbara send the two girls off to Barbara's uncle Roger's farm in Wisconsin, so they can play with their cousins during the summer. Don and Barbara are alone at last!

Now, Don and Barbara begin to feel guilt and anger, because the Court has taken away their son. Their discussions about Nat become increasingly heated and violent, initially verbally; then physically. On two occasions, Barbara calls 911 and asks for police assistance.

The more frequent the calls become, the closer the Police Officers are to jailing somebody.

Finally, Don and Barbara called me. You guessed it: I am the lucky Probation Officer assigned to this case. The parents want me to go to Sunny Horizons Boys Ranch, terminate Nat's placement there, and bring their kid back home. I tell them we will set a Court date, and discuss all the options with His Honor. I tell them that at the Court hearing, I will present the Court with my written Report to the Court and with a recommendation as to what I believe would be the most desirable outcome. I tell them that the RTC will present its report, and a recommendation as well.

I tell them that Nat and his Court-appointed Attorney will also be heard. Indeed, Children's services, if involved (and they very often are) may be heard, and, if one has been appointed by the Court, Nat's Guardian Ad Litem may be heard. Then, of course, the child's parents, and finally, if deemed appropriate by the Court, possibly the child's victim(s) as well will be heard. The Judge will then decide.

Here are some of the outcomes I have experienced:

The Judge will most often decide Nat can go home, even though no one except the parents believes (hopes) he is ready to leave the Treatment Center. This will, unfortunately, be the outcome most often during the final months of a Fiscal Year when placement funds are always short, to nonexistent. Every year during my career, my Department's Placement Budget for both Juvenile and

Adult Offenders was out of funds within five months into every Fiscal Year.

If Nat goes home, he will quickly become the center of family discord once again. The pressure of guilt is now at least partially, temporarily, off Don and Barbara, and they feel, temporarily, the relief of not being as intensively forced to examine their relationship. Nat will now revert to the rule expected of him within the family structure: he is once again belligerent, rebellious and destructive. He will soon be arrested once again and, as often as not, given this all-too-common scenario, Nat will be committed to the State Department of Corrections.

As a variation on that theme, Don, and Barbara move the family out of town or out of this State. Within two months, authorities from their new location will be contacting me, asking for copies of my Court File on Nat.

A better variation occasionally can occur, if Don and Barbara decide this family war has to stop. They may send Nat to live with uncle Roger (what a wonderful guy Roger is!) and his sisters, who are already with uncle Roger, while they go to their local version of "Doctor Phil," and try to get their marriage back together. When the children return, all family members may be refreshed, emotionally rearmed, and ready to be a well-functioning family. It has happened; not all that often, but I have seen it happen.

Suppose the Judge decides instead that Nat must stay at the Residential Treatment Center; what happens then?

Given that scenario, hopefully, everyone will accept the Judge's decision, hunker down and get back to work. The parents, hopefully, decide that the Residential Treatment

Center staff is their valuable ally. They cooperate. They let Nat know that he must go to work with the RTC, and his parents or he is "history." I have seen remarkable things happen under this scenario.

On the darker side, Nat conspires with Don and Barbara to undermine Nat's program at the RTC. This occurs far more often than anyone would want to see. Most of these facilities are largely unsecured. Nat can run off easily.

The staff probably will not be willing to strong-arm anyone into change. In this case, Nat may find himself ultimately committed to the State Department of Corrections. And, at that unhappy point, Don and Barbara will blame the entire sad state of affairs on, of course, yours truly, Kurt Niemann.

# THE NATURALIST

When I first saw eleven-year-old Kathleen ("Kitty") Hauser I was hooked by her broad, toothy smile and her bright eyes. What a shame she was in Detention.

Kitty would shoplift, even if she knew every cop in Cordova City was watching. By the time my office partner was assigned to her case, her Court Delinquency File was extensive, and her Children's Services Court File had been open for a total of six years. Kitty was, at least on paper, still being supervised by Children's Services. She had been Court-ordered into several foster homes since she was five years of age. Now, at this point,

Kitty being eleven years of age, the Judge ordered my office partner to explore the option of placement of Kitty in a "Group Home," of whatever appropriate stripe.

My partner, Barclay ("Barker") Lawrence, wanted me to meet Kitty while she was still in Detention, then also accompany him for a home visit. "I've heard some disturbing stuff," said Barker, "and I think I want a witness when I go to Kitty's house." There being nothing else critical or exciting than going on for me, I agreed to join him.

I accompanied Barker in his car to Kitty's parents' home. At first glance, I thought the property resembled an In-Country burned-out bunker. The grounds were scattered with various kinds of junk and debris. There was a door-less (Thank God!) refrigerator, an old water heater, a badly broken plastic bathtub, a few rusted-out cars, and at least one dead dog.

The house had a few windows still intact. There was no door attached to the front entrance. We exited Barker's car and approached the front entrance.

At ten feet from the door, I smelled the very strong stench of death. I told Barker that I was finished; I saw no need to inspect the interior of this house.

Barker entered the house. He and a woman, whom I assumed was Kitty's mother, exchanged a few pleasantries, and then he quickly exited the house.

I looked inside the house as well as I could from my location. The place was a shambles, beyond unfit for anything's habitation. I followed Barker to his car. He squatted down alongside his car and retched. He looked up at me and said: "I think my nose is broken forever."

The condition of the home helped us understand Kitty's ear and skin infections. What we could not understand was why the three children, all wards of Children's Services at that time, were still residing in the home, excepting, of course, Kitty. Barker began searching for an appropriate group home. Within two weeks one was located, and it was within one hundred miles of Cordova City.    The Court placed Kitty on Juvenile Probation, in the custody of the Residential Treatment Facility Barker had found. I was glad that being concerned over how long Kitty would be able to live in this clean and educational RTC was not my job.

Then, Barker did the unthinkable and unforgivable: He married the daughter of a Politically Prominent Real Estate VIP in Cordova Coty and resigned from his position with the Probation Department. So what, you say? Well, that meant Kitty's case went to my Caseload.

My first activity, in this case, was to contact the County Health Department and cry to these Authorities regarding Kitty's family home. To the eternal credit of those folks, the house was immediately condemned. At last, Children's Services found itself needing to foster out Kitty's two siblings.

Now, according to standard protocol, we needed to plan and prepare for family reunification. I can hear you saying: these parents need some help, including education regarding home cleanliness and proper hygiene. I agree. Now, as it so happened, Kitty's mother was a registered nurse. Kitty's stepfather was a chef at a local, high-priced, restaurant. What would you suggest they could not have known regarding sanitation?

Kitty did remain with the Residential Treatment Center for nearly two years. Ultimately, custody of Kitty was given to a maternal aunt and uncle in another State, where she remained, happily, at least until her reaching the age of adulthood.

Here is a wonderful anecdote about Kitty while with the RTC: Kitty was very intelligent, and once she was cleaned up, she began to excel in her schoolwork. She had an intense interest in all aspects of Flora and Fauna. She read books on geography and wildlife in the RTC's school library. She loved the Residential Center's National Geographic magazines and videotapes.

At one point, while living at the RTC, Kitty had found a pet lizard. She caught the lizard and made a cage for it of twigs and string. She told me she fed crickets to the lizard. I have no idea how she cared for the lizard. I do, however, recall the day she lost the lizard.

Kitty's Residential Treatment Center called me to say that Kitty was missing---again. We were becoming accustomed, and perhaps a bit overly tolerant, of Kitty's well-planned "Hide And Seek" games with the RTC staff. This time, the RTC Director was unhappy. He asked if I would help in the search. I agreed to do this. It took me a little over an hour to get to the RTC. Fortunately, by that time, Kitty had returned.

Usually, when Kitty was missing, she was hiding somewhere on the RTC campus. It was, as I said, an ongoing Game with her. She loved the Game. The RTC staff did not like the game at all, but they loved Kitty and they did their best to live with the frustration Kitty generated for them.

On a particular day, the center had asked me to assist in the search, Kitty had been seen to be walking off-campus by a schoolteacher. The teacher asked Kitty where she was going. Kitty told her that her pet lizard had escaped and that she was hunting it down. The teacher then informed Kitty that, retrieve the lizard or not, Kitty needed to be knocking on the principal's office door within a half-hour; if not, Police would be called in, and Kitty may find herself in Juvenile Detention once again.

The center director told me that Kitty knocked on the principal's office door within twenty minutes: with a lizard in Kitty's cage!

Kitty swore to me that this lizard was her very, heretofore missing, lizard. She explained that she had read that in the desert, a lizard's home has two holes: an entry hole and an escape hole in case of danger. She said she sought out and located the hole in the ground she believed her lizard had run into. She said she figured that this must have been her lizard's original home and that it had subsequently returned to when it escaped from her.

She then looked for another nearby "lizard hole." She then converted her lizard cage into a lizard trap and placed it at one of the holes. She packed dirt into the other hole. She jumped up and down on the ground between the two holes. The lizard ran out of the open hole, and into the trap.

Say what you will about this event; I saw a lizard in her lizard cage.

## THE "HAIR DANCE"

I have very little first-hand experience with the expensive "Boarding Schools" and "Military Academies" for children attending school up through grade 12. I do choose to believe that there are very legitimate reasons for many such placements of children, ranging from a child's "special needs" to an outright need for a child to discover oneself and to learn self-discipline.

I have heard from many educators and family therapists that these schools can also have a reputation as being "Detention Homes for the wealthy." I can appreciate how that could be true as well. I will suggest that when a child's behavior is out of control, regardless of the causality, it would be wonderful to be so economically secured as to be able to afford services Mr. Average cannot begin to hope for. That having been stated, I will argue that if a private citizen is going to contract with a private agency to provide boarding and educational services for a minor child, the placing citizen must discover as much as is possible regarding the agency and its' program.

While still assigned to Department's Section dealing with Status Offenders, I was assigned a case of a sixteen-year-old "Incorrigible" girl. I was ordered, by none other than our Presiding Judge, to present myself at Cordova City's Nimitz International Airport to meet this girl at her incoming flight, handcuff her and, with Betty Scott, a Transportation Officer, accompanying me, escort her to our West Side Juvenile Detention Facility.

My involvement with this "Inky" began the way it did because the sixteen-year-old girl's father was a prominent psychiatrist and also a State Legislator. This gentleman used his influence and the influence of his attorney to cause his daughter to be adjudicated "Incorrigible," in absentia, while the girl was still residing in an out-of-State private boarding school.

I never met with, nor did I ever converse with, her father. That gentleman, his attorney, and the Judge agreed that I was to speak only with the girl, when necessary, and to the father's attorney, but only when he called me.

The Department's mission with this girl was, per the Presiding Judge, to hold the girl until her father was able to successfully contract with another boarding school, or a similar, private of course, residential placement.

Her father did eventually locate and contract with another out-of-State boarding school. On the day appointed for the girl's departure from Detention, the Transportation Officer and I escorted her to the airport to meet her flight out. Upon a Motion filed by the father's attorney, the Court dismissed the "Incorrigible" case.

What made this case particularly interesting to me was the information that I was given regarding staff behavior at the girl's former boarding school.

In discussing life at her former boarding school, some of the girl's complaints to me, particularly her allegations regarding "The Hair Dance," sounded a bit exaggerated at first. However, it happened that there were, at the time, employed among our Detention staff, two men and a woman who had been employed at that school, and who also knew this girl. They confirmed to me that the girl was truthful in her description of the school's disciplinary methods.

In order to conduct "The Hair Dance," the staff of this school will circle the targeted "acting out" child. Then, one staff member will purchase, if possible with both hands, the child's hair. That staff member will then jerk the child around by the hair until it is believed by the staff that the child has become willing to stop his or her "inappropriate" behavior.

It happens that this boarding school is owned and operated by a religious organization.

One further note: shortly before I retired I had to mention this school's use of "The Hair Dance" to a clergyman belonging to the same religious organization which operates that school. His response was "So, what's wrong with that?"

Okay, I guess I just don't get it.

# PREVENTING A CRISIS IS EXPENSIVE

During my years of being responsible for the Juvenile Detention Officer's Academy, I maintained a sharp interest in inmate/student/client maltreatment, particularly regarding incidents involving injuries or deaths.

Being responsible for training new Officers, I believed it to be of primary importance to train staff in methodologies around preventing crises. Failing prevention of a crisis, staff must also be well trained in crisis resolution methodologies likely to prevent or minimize injury to inmates and staff.

When I opened the Department's Detention Officers Academy, I trusted that our Chief Administrators would support Academy efforts to prevent injuries, physical damage, and litigation. In general, administrators do tend to at least verbalize appreciation of these lofty goals, at least so long as their budgets are not adversely affected, meaning so long as training does not interfere with other, agendas viewed as more pressing at the time. In reality, staff training tends to be the stepchild of any organization. Rather than being proactive, training programs usually developed as reactions to the most recent crisis.

On almost every day, the Good Guys win in the Police and Corrections fields. This is because in most cases, people screened in during the hiring process begin their employment loaded with high professional aspirations. It also helps that in their hiring and promotion processes, Criminal justice agencies are increasingly demanding higher levels of formal education and experience.

All that having been noted, what follows is a short list intended to illustrate a few more red flags of danger I have seen or read about in this country during the final dozen years of my career.

# WHIPPING THEM INTO SHAPE

Billy Miller found his way onto my Probation Caseload by pleading guilty to a charge of indecent exposure. He entered his Guilty Plea in two dramatically different arenas: Initially, at Juvenile Court, then, at the insistence of the family Pastor, during a church service, before the entire assembly of the church congregation. These episodes proved to be an embarrassing series of events, indeed for this young man: the offense he had committed was that he had gone to the Cordova City Downtown Branch Library, checked out a copy of Gray's Anatomy, sat at a reading table, and was observed by the Librarian to be masturbating.

I was in the courtroom when, as part of the entry of a plea of guilty, Billy described his transgression to the judge. The kid was devastated. I am very glad that I did not have to be present when he was made, as per the rules of his church, to stand before his congregation and confess once more.

Several weeks later, the Judge placed Billy Miller on probation. He was then assigned to yours truly.

Very soon after being placed on Probation, Billy's parents notified me that they were going to send their Young Sinner to a church-operated boarding school, "For a while." They let me know that I should encounter no difficulty securing from the Court the necessary one thousand dollars weekly church boarding school fee, the cost of Billy being with them, because, their Pastor had told them, "The Court always pays for this sort of thing."

I then donned my best Diplomat's Hat and explained to Mr. And Mrs. Miller the ins and outs of securing Court funds for rehabilitation services for juvenile and adult probationers. Mr. And Mrs. Miller were kind enough to let me know that their Pastor had predicted that I would say what I did, but that what I had just said was in reality only a "verbal smokescreen." Their Pastor had told them that all they had to do was stand firm with their demand, and I would have no choice but to secure the funds for them.

I do not recall how many dozens of times I'd been faced with desperate, earnest, and well-meaning citizens very much like the Millers, so terribly misinformed by people they held in high esteem, e.g., persons of the Cloth, therapists, Public School Officials, et al. I know I have cited at least one other, similar, case earlier in this book. I could always tell when this particular "You're Lying To Me" Litany was on the way from the citizen's mouth: the eyelids would flutter, the eyes would glaze over and they would repeat in a deadpan manner what they had been told to tell me.

What a crock. I wonder how often professional people, working with families having problems such as those faced by the Millers, send these folks to me simply as a way to get rid of them. And, However, in all fairness, I have come realize that sometimes pastors/counselors/school officials/attorneys/doctors or whoever, often truly believe these fallacies, having themselves been misinformed by an Authority that they, themselves, respected and believed.

And, sometimes people in the helping professions can be reluctant to admit that they do not know the facts.

Compounding the problems people face with knowing and understanding "The real facts" around placements, and who pays for them, are the constant program and budget changes going on, with the RTC's, the Courts, insurance companies, and philanthropic organizations. Just within the Court systems, policies and budgets can be sufficiently bizarre and/or irrational that "The truth" can be difficult to discover and understand.

Anyway, it also happened that Mr. And Mrs. Miller had been misleading me (Gasp!) as to Billy's actual whereabouts. They had given custody of Billy well in advance of notifying me and asking for Court assistance, and now they expected the Court to pay somewhat more than one thousand dollars per week, no questions asked.

Could the situation be much worse than this for the P.O. to handle? Of course, it could be---and it was. This Residential Placement, while in our State at the time Billy was placed, was located outside our County, and it was not on the Official State "Approved" list with either the Courts or the Children's Services Agency. The Residential Placement Staff, From the Groundskeeper up to the Director, and including the Board, were already under investigation at that time by an impressive number of State licensing and Law Enforcement agencies, as a result of numerous and various allegations of physical brutality, allegedly regularly inflicted upon their young Charges.

Among other nightmare stories being circulated, several former residents were saying that corporal punishment was routine, and always applied with loud prayer. For example, it was alleged that one of the staff's corporal punishments was to tie a resident offender to a post, and then to beat the offender with a whip, while passages from the Bible were being read aloud.

Preposterous? All lies, you say, being told by the Godless Media and disgruntled Probation Officers? Ah, but there's more:

The Judge was not thrilled to hear my report on the Miller family's actions regarding Billy. The Judge ordered a "Probation Review" Hearing, and Mr. and Mrs. Miller was ordered to be present at that hearing. The Judge also ordered the Millers to bring their son Billy to the hearing with them.

At the appointed day and time, the Millers appeared in Court, but without Billy. When questioned by the Judge, Mr. Miller elected to, essentially, "stonewall" the Court. Mr. Miller claimed that he did not have to respond to the Judge. He claimed that "Maritime Law" empowered him to defy the Court. He claimed that under "Maritime Law," the Constitution of The United States and the laws of our State are invalid. He made these statements while reading from a notepad in his hand, never once looking at the Judge. Stating to the Court that his Pastor had armed him with this knowledge, he defied Court to touch him or his son, Billy. Then he and his wife paraded out of the Courtroom.

During my career, I encountered perhaps six cases involving people who would invoke "Maritime Law" as authority to deny recognition of U.S. laws and Courts. As a Probation Officer, I found these people to be a lot of fun to watch in court. Judges and Attorneys, however, do not enjoy these whackos at all. I recall a case when such a screaming defendant invited the Judge to do his worst. He was still screaming as the Sheriff's Deputies led him away, handcuffed, to jail, on a "contempt" citation. Defying the Court can bring about harsh consequences.

Shortly following that Probation Review Hearing, Billy Miller was spirited, by the church operated RTC, out of our State, then placed in a series of further newly-opened, but short-lived, the church operated Residential Centers; first in a neighboring State, then in a State further east, and, finally, in a State deep within the Bible-Belt South, still with the same church folks to whom his parents had assigned physical custody. These church-run "Children's Homes" were being ejected by State Courts from State to State, due to their "alleged" refusal to adhere to even the most basic tenets of humane and therapeutic child care and treatment. Still, the Millers refused to recall Billy, saying, "He's in the hands of the Lord." During this time, the RTC accountants faithfully billed the Court every month for Billy's care and maintenance. Naturally, we did not respond to these billing notices.

At last, the church-operated children's homes in which Billy Miller had been residing were beginning to attract the attention of news media nationwide.

First, children's advocacy groups, and then more Government and civil legal authorities became aware and outraged by the actions of the RTC staff.

Investigations were ordered by Children's Service Agencies and by Juvenile Courts. Their findings were no surprise to those of us who had been following this group. Here were a few of those findings:

The children's meals generally were a mixture of rice, grits, and oats, sometimes with other leftover scraps from prior meals mixed in. I was told by that State's Legal Authorities that the children spent the majority of each day performing hard fieldwork, including harvesting crops, digging ditches, dismantling nearby abandoned buildings, and using the resulting materials to build "new" structures on the property of the Children's Home. There were lengthy morning and evening prayer meetings: these meetings also served as "school." The children were allowed no media of any sort, printed or electronic, not even music: all printed and electronic media was declared by the church to be "The work of The Devil."

No violations of Camp Rules were tolerated. There were, I was told, no "second chances;" no warnings beyond the children's first-day orientation. Offenders were beaten, sometimes I was told, by the Camp's Pastor;

And sometimes the Camp Pastor assigned an older juvenile Resident to this duty.

My Presiding Judge ordered me to devote my full time to investigating this organization, at least as well as I was capable of doing so, being hundreds of miles away from the RTCs' locations. The Judge ordered me to deliver my Report to him in no more than two weeks.

I contacted juvenile officials in three of that State's Counties. Naturally, they were initially guarded in their conversations with me, since I was an unknown outsider. However, following their background investigations on me, I was able to garner comments from them such as these:

"We will never send a child there. There are an extreme church and state conflicts and those people inflict corporal punishment upon the children."

"…Also, we will deny providing you with Courtesy Supervision of any of your Wards placed there, should you request it . . ."

"There are significant amounts of legal and physical difficulties with the Camps and with the Camp's staff . . ."

Ironically, what finally caused the State to close down the residences (there were a few for boys and a few for girls) was action precipitated by an official of another Christian church. This man, a Bishop, had a church located very near one of the Camps. I was told that as his suspicions regarding these Camps grew, he contacted Camp staff and made inquiries. He was told by the Camp staff to mind the business of his church and to stay out of theirs. At that time, he elected to contact State and Local Authorities and the news media. When I spoke with this man his voice frequently cracked and wavered, he was so outraged by the actions in which the adults in these Homes engaged against the children "allegedly In the name of the Lord." Soon after my conversation with the

Bishop, some of the chief officials of the Children's Home staff had been arrested. The homes were condemned and closed. Those children, who for various reasons could not be immediately sent to their parental homes, became Wards of the State and were fostered. Billy Miller was returned to his parents. Mr. and Mrs. Miller blamed the entire debacle on me; no surprise. They immediately sent Billy to yet another "Christian Academy." I have no idea as to who was footing the bill for Billy's new placement; my Court certainly was not. Upon my recommendation, the Court washed its hands of the Miller family. When I telephoned the Miller residence to inform them of the Court's decision, Mrs. Miller told me: "the Lord will always win over people like you."

## BOOT CAMPS

If you have seen the movie "Full Metal Jacket," you have seen what I will call an excellent portrayal of my own U.S. Marine Corps Boot Camp training. However, mine took place quite a few years earlier, during 1956, at the Marine Corps Recruit Depot in California, at that time located in San Diego. Semper Fi!

Unlike the movie Full Metal Jacket, I did not shoot my drill instructor; nor can I imagine the remotest possibility of such an incident occurring at a Marine Corps Recruit Depot. I'm certain the thought did cross my mind, as, I am sure, may have been true for a number of my fellow Boots in Recruit Platoon 2025, Gunnery Sergeant Louis

H. Lazarko commanding. I am certain, however, that no one, myself included, seriously considered carrying out this fantasy, If for no other reason than I knew that this training, difficult though it might have been to experience as a seventeen-year-old boy, was going to save my life if I were to be exposed to combat. Well, perhaps the primary reason that I did not seriously consider attempting to harm Gunny Lazarko was that I believed that any attempt to do so would only piss him off and I would end up "Falling over a locker box" several times, then be sent to Sick Bay, then to the Brig, where unsympathetic guards would probably cause me to severely regret having been born!

To summarize my own Boot Camp experience, I thank God for the education and the maturation I received from Gunny Lazarko and the Marine Corps. So, where am I going with all this?

The Boot Camp in which I was trained and became a Marine was owned and operated by a United States Government Military organization. That Boot Camp employed professional, well-trained, career members of the most elite military organization in the world.

Parents by the hundreds, frustrated by the inability to control their teenagers and angry that the State cannot or will not help, call the U.S. Military, as my mother did, or the many and various "Military Academies" catering to elementary and high school-aged children so plentiful in the United States.

Some families, being less well endowed financially, contact privately owned and operated "boot camps." They do this because it is "Conventional Wisdom" in our American culture that "Boot Camp will straighten him out and make a man out of him!"

In the case of the U.S. Military, not every kid that walks into a Recruiting Station will qualify, physically and/or emotionally, to be selected to go to a U.S. Military Boot Camp. In addition, not every New Recruit entering into a Boot Camp will successfully graduate. For example, in my outfit, Platoon 2025, eighty Recruits started; only fifty-five of us graduated.

In the case of the established civilian Military Academies in the United States, many of these Academies for elementary and high school-aged youngsters have been around for a hundred years or more, and most do provide first-class academic and behavioral education. At the same time, one must be very cautious as to which children should attend this kind of setting, and which children should not. I'll wager my pension that these Academies are also very cautious and selective during the pre-enrollment process, very much in the same way, and for much the same reasons, as are our Armed Services. A lot of stress and a lot of discipline awaits the student at a Military Academy.

I wish parents would be equally cautious and selective when considering privately owned and operated "boot camps," which advertise behavior modification programs as roughly (no pun intended) of the "Tough Love" genre for the children.

Criminal and civil litigation has been ongoing for years, concerning the incredible deaths of a number of teenagers in "boot camps" or "survival camps," in my State and many other States as well. A number of these "boot camps" have been ordered closed by the Courts over the past several years. Here are but a few examples:

In Maryland, the Governor of that State released a report finding "Twenty-nine possible cases of excessive force, child abuse, or simple assault" in that State's private "boot camps."

A fifteen-year-old Texas boy died of heatstroke with which he was stricken during a "one-day boot camp."

The U.S. Department of Justice criticized the state of Georgia for allowing boot camps in that State, which were "not only ineffective but harmful." The State of Georgia shut them all down.

Did I hear you say: "Juvenile boot camps will work if the various States' Departments of Juvenile Corrections will operate them?" Well, let's look at the record:

The U.S. Department of Justice has investigated and is monitoring the South Dakota Department of Juvenile Corrections. A two hundred twenty pound, fourteen-year-old, the girl was forced to run over two miles on her first day at South Dakota's State-run boot camp. After being left lying in the sun for three hours, she was transported to a hospital where she died of hypothermia.

Other girls were forced to run while shackled.

The Sioux Falls newspaper reported, "Teenage girl inmates were strip-searched by male guards." Others were pepper-sprayed while naked. Others were shackled, spread-eagle, on beds, blindfolded and their clothes cut off--- by male guards---, according to a report in my files.

A counselor in another South Dakota camp was accused of molesting six boys.

Considering the above, it can come as no surprise that during the year 2000, a Federal class-action lawsuit was filed against the state of South Dakota.

In 1998, the Juvenile Justice Project of Louisiana and the Mental Health Association of Louisiana filed a Federal Lawsuit against the state's Juvenile Corrections Department, alleging numerous physical and mental abuses and neglect.

All told, at the time of my retirement in 2001, at least the following states were being similarly investigated: Arizona, California, Delaware, Florida, Georgia, Illinois, Louisiana, Maryland, South Dakota, Texas, and Virginia.

Now, that's what I would call: Whipping Them Into Shape!

*Chapter VII*

# THE ACADEMY

## INTRODUCTION:

Here was my Golden Opportunity to substantially impact the juvenile part of the justice system in my state: I was assigned the tasks of creating and operating our first Juvenile Detention Officers Training Academy! This part of my career spanned my final five years. Not one moment with the Academy was humdrum.

## CREATING THE ACADEMY

As of the year 2000, according to my research, nearly every adult jail and prison featured some kind of new employee training program. This is not true of all the Juvenile Justice System's Probation Officers and Detention officers.

Perhaps this does not seem as strange and inappropriate to the reader as it does to this writer. In the first place, if I were King of all Criminal Justice System Budgets, the lion's share of annual monies would go to the State's various Juvenile Justice Agencies. This is because I strongly believe that If there is to be hope in turning around the thousands of years of the world's various failures at preventing or changing criminal behavior, it will have to begin with addressing the younger generations. Adult Corrections Agencies nationwide have been famous over the decades for being a Primary State Budget "Money Pit," with few results toward preventing recidivism.

At the same time, Juvenile programs receive proportionally far less funding.

Although academic education beyond a High School diploma or G.E.D is not required of staff in the majority of this Country's Juvenile lockups, in my State the entry-level positions begin with a requirement of an A.A., or sixty-four units of college credit. At the same time, few State and County-operated juvenile lockups have pre-service academic training programs for new employees in the Juvenile field. In fact, in 1996, I was assigned the duty of writing the first Juvenile Detention Officer's Pre-Service Academy in my State.

During the 1980s and 1990s, I was my Agency's most often utilized Crisis Prevention and Intervention instructor, assigned by my Agency to be trained and certified by one of the National Crisis Intervention Programs within the United States. As I have mentioned earlier in this book, I have experienced precious little cause to develop respect for most of the heavily touted and grandly marketed nationwide training programs for the area of dealing with violently acting out persons. The program for which I was ordered by the State to be certified as an instructor did contain a very realistic program in verbal intervention techniques. However, the total program, as is true in my opinion, of nearly all the rest of similar programs currently available, had very little practical substance to offer in terms of staff self-defense and relatively non-injurious inmate restraint techniques.

This area of staff training was and remains of primary importance to me due to the understanding of this area I have developed through my martial arts background. Because of this background, it is evident to me that, in the area of physical interventions, most of the techniques offered in these programs range from inadequate to outright bogus. For years I verbally hammered at my Administration to allow me to create a better training program. I suppose that after a number of my speeches and memos, my superiors came to expect my periodic ritual requests. I must say that I never actually expected a positive response from the Executive Offices to the extent of being asked to create an entire Detention Officer Training Program!

Then, one day in August 1996, the Juvenile Detention Director walked into my office, took a chair, grinned, and asked: "Niemann, can you write an Academy for me?"

Always ready to play a verbal Game, I replied: "Sure. I can have a Juvenile Detention Officer's Academy written and operating within three or four months."

The director grinned and said: "Great! You've got three months. I want the first forty complete Juvenile Detention Officer's Academy Training Manuals on my desk in six weeks. And, at that time I also want a list of people you think should be teaching along with you in the Academy!"

Just like that. After all these years of, I suppose, begging, for a far lesser opportunity, here was the Brass Ring!

My choices for Academy trainers included Mamasita and Willie, the two Officers who had been my partners in Detention for quite a while, and Curly, who had recently retired from the Police Department. This was because I'd been discussing my training issues with these three Officers for a long time, and we were all in agreement as to the problems and possible solutions.

Excellent resources for writing the Academy Training Manual and the general curriculum were plentiful. We dealt with adolescent behavior, liability issues, report writing, addictions, first aid, and CPR, preventing and dealing with crises, and a host of other subjects. I found wonderful tapes on sexual harassment issues, the Stanford/Zimbardo study, and, of course, we always presented to the classes selected scenes from the movies, <u>One Flew Over The Cuckoo's Nest. (Remember Nurse Ratched?) and West Side Story (Remember Dear Officer Krupke?)</u>

The first Juvenile Detention Officer's Academy did open just three months after the Detention Director had given me the green light. The remaining years of my career in the Criminal Justice System were served in the capacity of operating this Academy. The job was a pure delight.

Well, at least, most of the time.

# THE PLAYERS

In most cases, the new Juvenile Detention Officer's Academy would open with a majority of young people, mostly with A.A. Degrees; some with Bachelors and even Master's Degrees. Few had any real experience dealing with juveniles at all, much fewer delinquents. That, in my opinion, was usually so much the better.

There were always a few new employees on the other end of the age and experience spectrum – retired military, a few retired priests and nuns, former

U.S. Postal Service people, teachers, real estate people - - -a healthy cross-section of our adult population.

There were also professional ballplayers. We had pro-basketball, baseball, and, mostly, football people, all hired on a part-time or "on-call" basis, of course. They were always a great group of young men and women, usually joining us as a sort of "payback" to the Community and hoping to positively influence the troubled juveniles in our Detention Facilities.

The professional ballplayers also tended to be a positive influence on other staff members within our Agency as well; the older staff experiencing "burnout" in particular. I have never been a particular fan of "spectator sports;"

however, I did become an ardent fan of professional ballplayers. In many ways, their "Gung Ho" attitudes reminded me of my Brothers and Sisters in the Marine Corps. I never heard them swear (I wish the same could be said of myself); I never saw one professional ballplayer lose his or her temper. And, yes, they certainly did positively influence the juveniles.

In my opinion, one professional ballplayer in a Juvenile Detention Facility can do more to turn around a gangbanger than can a dozen other Professionals of most other suits.

The Players did tend, of course, to be playful, including on the job. At the same time, they were, for the most part, sensitive and expert in knowing when and where to "draw the line" when working in the cellblocks.

The players also liked to have fun in the Academy, which generally was fine with me, since I was the least likely Academy Instructor to be demanding total solemnity in the classrooms. My basic rules for classroom instruction are: Leave your Ego at the door and bring a sense of humor in with you.

One Player, while having fun in the Academy did encounter an "oops" neither of us will likely forget, and I am grateful for the good nature of the perpetrator:

It was Crisis Prevention and Verbal and Physical Intervention Techniques week. We were entering into hands-on training involving prevention of grabs, front/rear/sides, and countering of grabs. We always created "partners" and "teams" for this training in the Academy and, of course, we always emphasized starting into learning these techniques softly, slowly, and very, very carefully.

By the time of this phase in Academy training, for most Academy students, if there had been any doubts that this sixty-year-old Instructor was an experienced Martial Artist, those doubts were by now fairly dispelled. Most students respected me or at least respected my skills, and they respected Curly, who was trained in Aikido, as well.

This having been outlined, Players will be Players: during one class lecture break on particular, one of those enormous human tanks they call Linebackers grabbed me from behind in a very snug bear hug.

BIG MISTAKE! As a result of decades of training, without hesitation, I stepped out into a "low horse" to my right and my left hand delivered a "knife-edge" blow to the rear, connecting solidly with the man's groin. He fell without a sound.

I did what I did totally as a trained reaction; it was nothing personal. When the six-and-one-half foot, three-hundred-pound Linebacker picked himself up from the floor, he had a grin on his face and he said "Hey, Niemann, you're not bad for an old fart!"

## THE POUTERS

I did encounter a few dissatisfied customers in the Juvenile Detention Officer's Academy. They were, thank God, the minority by far, but they did at times create serious heartburn for instructors and classmates alike.

On the first day of each new academy, I handed out manuals, curriculum, progress expectations, dress, and behavior expectations. Yep, got to report in every morning. Yep, got to participate in class. Nope, no shorts, miniskirts, plunging necklines, and bras must be worn (except for the men). Yep, there will be a mid-term, written, exam and a final, written exam (loud groan from the class).

From which corner of the Devil's Department of Idiocy comes the popular belief among new employees that progress checks (that's "tests" to you) are an outrage, offensive, and a violation of Federal EEOC rules? Yes, I am aware that America's education system does appear to pander to the

Intellectually Lowest Common Denominator. So, just how untrained and untested are you willing for your Criminal Justice System's various Officers to be? How about your airline pilot? How about Your Neurosurgeon? Who will you hold responsible if your accountant, your attorney, your self-defense instructor, or your automotive repair technician is incompetent, as a consequence of that incompetence, causes you injury?

After the culture shock of the first day at the Academy, most new employees deal with the emotional trauma I have created and move on. Once in a while, however, a new hire will be spooked by the thought of being held accountable and will stop attending within a few more days. For both the new dropout and for the Agency, this will have been a good decision.

I do recall while going through the Graduate School "rite of passage" at the university I attended, I detested the professors who would seek out remote, nitpicky passages in footnotes or from some centuries-old bibliography, and use this data for creating "Gotcha" questions in written Class examinations.

Consequently, my written tests for the Academy were made up of material which for the most part you could not have missed if you attended class, paid reasonable attention took a few notes and was not too seriously stoned.

Nonetheless, in every class, there would always appear that "Ten Percent;" those who, it would appear, could pass a written exam only if the sole question asked was for the correct spelling of the student's name. Teachers and students worldwide would recognize all the lame excuses I used to love to hear:

"I didn't know there was a test." "I can't take a test."

"You never talked about any of that." "I have a sleeping disorder (!)." "I'm pregnant."

"The classroom was too hot/too cold." "They were all trick questions."

"You can't test me, I'm already hired!"

"You didn't have any 'extra credit' questions." "My period started."

"My girlfriend's period hasn't started."

The best, and the worst, Academy students were those who had been with us, working in our Juvenile Detention Facilities for one year or less, and now needed, by order of the Chief, to attend the Academy. Most were happy to attend and were very beneficial to the Academy classes. They would have had sufficient experience to share ideas and opinions we often decided to retain for future Academies. However, the "Ten Per centers" either glared or stared at us, arms and legs crossed, thereby often hastening their termination. I called these folks "The Pouters."

The Queen of the Pouters of all the Academy classes I ran was one Heather Macmillan. Heather, the oldest daughter of one of the Probation Department Directors, had at one time been one of our Probation Officers, but she left us after two years of employment. The lady resigned, I believed, after finding no end to the line of colleagues who disliked her negative views of all people, places, and things. She did ultimately return, applying one year later for employment as a Juvenile Detention Officer. She, therefore, was required to attend the Juvenile Detention Officer's Academy.

Heather began the academy by informing us that she already knew more about the job than anyone else in the Department save, of course, her mother and the Chief. Moreover, she said, everything in the Academy Training Manual and the Academy Curriculum was incorrect.

Heather and another young lady, whose mind ran along the same arrogant and negative path as Heather's, sat through the entire Academy in the front row, side by side, both slouched, legs and arms crossed, glaring at the various lecturers. It became a source of a great deal of humor on the part of the new employees. It is to the credit of my Academy Instructors that all kept a straight face given this buffoonery.

We did discuss giving the rest of the class extra credit for their tolerance of the two malcontents.

# THE PARAMEDIC

I always looked forward to our First aid/CPR day in the Academy. The instructor, Chuck Harris, was a Battalion Chief with the Cordova City Fire Department and a Licensed Paramedic.

Chuck's day always began with four hours, no breaks, of CPR training. Chuck provided all materials, including fourteen "Annie" CPR dummies, an adolescent CPR dummy, and an infant CPR dummy. Early on he also presented to myself and each of my other Academy Instructors a T-shirt; copies of the same bright-red-with-white-lettered "CPR Dummy" T-shirts the "Annie's" wore. I mean, is this "In" or what! The students heard a lecture, saw a movie, then he worked them. Then he worked them some more. Then he worked them again. Then he gave them a written test as well.

By lunchtime, my people knew CPR, they talked CPR; they were just waiting, hoping, for someone to fall so they could work CPR!

Chuck just had that kind of personality. He was a born leader with a commanding voice and a sense of humor that never went away.

One of my favorite stories of Chuck's adventures as a Paramedic with Cordova City Fire Department had to do with an evening when the Night Dispatch announced a 9-11 calls involving "a kid choking." Chuck and his crew strapped into the Fire Departments Life Support vehicle and raced, Code Three, to the address related by Dispatch.

Chuck's assigned area was partially rural, and this call was to a small farm. Upon arrival, he immediately recognized the farm, and then he recognized the owner of the farm, even though the owner was on his knees, his back to chuck, clearly administering CPR to - - a Kid.

The farm's owner, retired Cordova City Police Department Homicide Detective Ira Martinez, had been Chuck's close friend for several decades, both having been raised in the same area, gone to school together, and employed in Cordova City Public Safety Branches at the same time.

Ira Martinez, now a retired cop, now lived in comfort in a rural area and owned and operated a goat farm. And one of his Kids was choking. He was attempting CPR on the Kid when Chuck and his team arrived.

As Chuck's crew was reviving the Kid, Chuck began upbraiding Ira for deceiving Dispatch. Ira replied:

"Chuck, I didn't deceive Dispatch. I told the woman that one of my young Kids was choking. Would she have sent you out if I'd said I have a choking goat?"

Probably not.

A quick footnote here: I was fortunate enough to know Detective Ira Martinez as well; I had first met him during my rookie years. Ira was particularly proud of his several photo albums; they were replete with photos of all the homicide victims he'd dealt with to date. He always carried with him an album stuffed with photos of his most recent victims, some of which had been deceased, at the time of photographing, for several days, sometimes for weeks. Thanks to Ira, I learned the trick to being able to hold in one's lunch when working in a location permeated with the stench of rotting flesh. Just in case you may want to know, how it's done is: when one initially enters the infected area, one very slowly and deliberately takes three very deep breaths. Believe it or not, this works!

But, back to Chuck's First Aid Class. These classes typically had little or nothing to do with properly folding triangular bandages and students wrapping students like mummies. He taught my Academy students how to take a pulse, how to look for a concussion, how to prepare injured people for emergency medical personnel. He demonstrated how to stabilized a foreign object embedded in the body (eye, chest, neck, etc.). He emphasized minimum necessary items in your car for first aid: saran wrap, duct tape, and a magazine (no, not to read while waiting two hours for help, it's to roll up and use for a splint). He showed the ins and outs of sucking chest wounds and compound fractures. In short, he taught truly practical First Aid.

In a short time, Chuck's CPR/First Aid classes In Detention also became very popular with Adult and Juvenile Probation Officers and their support staff. There was always a waiting list for his classes. The State decreed that annual refresher classes in these subjects were mandatory, and he made learning, even of these relatively dry subjects, entertaining and therefore enjoyable. I wish there had been more instructors like him during all my various excursions into education, particularly during my Graduate School experience.

And how about those amputations? Chuck had seen countless amputations during his career. He would give the class all the information regarding plastic wraps, ice chests, and so on, and then he always told the Academy classes of a multi-vehicle accident he and his crew were called out on during his rookie years. It seems the driver of one of the cars involved had lost his left arm as a consequence of the collision. The arm was located by one of the Fire Department's Ambulance Service EMTs. The EMT raised the arm, pointed to the wristwatch still attached to the arm, and shouted:

"Takes a Lickin' and keeps on Tickin'!"

## HIGH STEPPIN'

I will tell you that your best self-defense technique, whenever possible, is the "Nike" method: you use your "Nike's" to get the hell away from your attacker.

This is a tough concept indeed for some people to accept in practice. No one with an ego larger than a walnut wants to be thought of as cowardly. That fear of being seen as "yellow" has been keeping hospital emergency rooms and dental surgeons busy for centuries.

The primary goal in the life of a true professional Martial Artist is to work toward creating a world without conflict. Sorry about that, all you wannabe Tough Guys. Genuine Martial Artists fight only when they have no other reasonable option left to them and when they need to protect themselves or their loved ones. I know, I know,

Hollywood will never hire me to create a "Hero" movie. My loss.

Nevertheless, this is an important concept for Police, Probation, and Corrections Officers, because nerves and emotions can become raw at any moment. A lot of inmates would rather not be residing in your particular "Bed And Breakfast" establishment (really!). Anger, fear, frustration, pain often is present, on both sides of the Badge. How much of this is so at any time is always a function, primarily, of two critical factors: first, the individual Criminal Justice Department's pre-employment selection policy, and its employee training policy and process; second, the conditions of the physical work environment.

Once more, it is my opinion that the vast majority of actual physical altercations between Officers and inmates, or suspects, resulting in injury and/or death, have most often either been initiated by or have been accelerated by, the Officers. Yes, there are exceptions, but very few.

Suspects and inmates are experts in goading insufficiently trained Officers into conflict. Officers, of course, do feel a need to not be "one-upped" by suspects and inmates. In any given case, an Officer's verbal and physical responses to folks who are trolling for trouble will be a function of the phenomenon called "Primary Default." What this means is that the officer's response will be a direct reflection of the quality and quantity of the officer's total training, and particularly his most recent training, if any.

How did we train our officers to avoid physical conflict? Here are some of the basic rules we had in the Academy:

Report for duty in good physical and emotional shape.

Before going on duty, discover what has transpired in your duty area while you've been gone.

If you're in charge of a cellblock, do what you can to set up the physical area so that potential conflicts are minimized as much as possible.

Always remember: you're in charge. Stay in charge. If you succumb to an inmate's games, the inmate will be in charge.

During the self-defense and physical restraint portions of our conflict prevention and resolutions classes, I used a number of methods to illustrate the value of avoidance of physical conflict. One of my favorite examples in the area of being in control and maintaining a professional image dealt with an exercise dealing with avoidance of kicks from an agitated person. Allow Academy Student Jasmine Gabriel to illustrate:

During the classes involving a lot of physical movement, the classroom would be empty of furniture. For this particular exercise, I would ask all the students to line up against one wall and observe the activity to follow. I would then ask for a volunteer, one who would be willing to kick this aged, out-of-shape Academy Instructor.

My volunteer during academy class 27 was Jasmine Gabriel. Jasmine was a tall, trim, clearly athletic, beauty. As she walked out of the center of the classroom, my partner, Curly, whispered in my ear, "Good Grief, Kurt, her legs alone are six feet tall!" If not exactly true, they must have been close.

My instructions to Jasmine, as with all volunteers in this particular activity, were as follows:

"Jasmine, when next I say the word "Go" I want you to kick me as hard as you can. If you miss, I want you to make an honest attempt to kick me again. I want you to keep kicking me until either Curly or I say: "Stop". Any questions?

Jasmine's smile was nearly as wide as the classroom. As a demonstration of what I had invited upon myself, she executed two practice "crescent" kicks, both higher than my head. Omigawd, she must be a Tae Kwan Do student! It did appear to be her goal to make this Old Guy lie down, and for a long time!

She told us she was ready. Curly was standing some twenty feet behind me. He appeared to be to ready give me CPR.

I shouted, "Go!" and then I quickly stepped back!

At the same time, Jasmine grinned, leaped forward while executing a "crescent" kick, and- - -Jasmine fell back, landing on her butt! She did not connect with me.

I said, quickly, "Stop."

At that point, I informed the class, and this remains true today, that no one on the street or in a cellblock has ever tried to kick me while jumping toward me and connected. I simply step back.

Oh, boy! I can hear it coming: "Yeah, but, Bruce Lee, or Kwai Chang Caine, or my friend Wunhung Lo, who is a grandmaster in the Ancient Art of Hu Flungdung; they can kick your butt!"

Well, yes, it certainly does help to have a movie scriptwriter be on your side. However, in real life, keep your Cool, and place your trust in your Nike's.

Even in a closed-in area, like a cellblock, all that is needed in this kind of case is to be out of range; appropriate Officer reaction can easily follow. I know this to be true: I've been there.

# BACK TO THE REZ

Early in my career, at the same time that Curly and I were busily eradicating gangs, for all eternity, from Cordova City, a certain Native American prostitute was arrested in the downtown, or Deuce, section.

This particular hooker was not arrested, however, for plying her trade.

Someone in the fleabag hotel in which she kept a room for herself, her black boyfriend/pimp, and her infant son, had told a Children's Services worker that this prostitute's child was both neglected and abused. A Children's Services Caseworker, with a Cordova City police escort, found the child living under conditions worse than a T.V. news producer at the time would dare display. Mama and her boyfriend were jailed, and the child went to a foster home.

Realizing that the child's mother would be soon released from jail, Curly and I helped with negotiations with her particular tribe's Chief of Social Services, who happened, fortunately, to be a long-time flying buddy of mine. Mother and child were accepted back onto the Reservation, with a proviso that her black boyfriend was not to move in with her. It had been the constant verbal and physical violence going on between mother and boyfriend that had resulted in their expulsion from the Reservation, some few years earlier.

Then, forwarding a few more years, those Fates, which love to laugh at Officers who become too comfortable with life, caused the Presiding Judge to call me regarding this family. This time, the identified problem was the child: he'd been arrested, in my old assigned gang area of course, on a charge of prostitution. This was none of my affairs, until the child's mom, remembering Niemann's ability to do magic, had asked the tribal Judge to cause me to be assigned her son's case.

So it came to be that, between my Academy classes, I engaged in telephone and face-to-face negotiations with Tribal Authorities (a two hundred sixty mile round trip each time we were face-to-face). I caused the young man to be released from jail and into a Halfway House setting, located on the Reservation.

He went on AWOL from the Halfway House, and soon was arrested once more, on a prostitution charge, in Cordova City.

I took him back to the Reservation. He left again, only to be arrested on attempted auto theft in a town close to the Reservation.

The Indian police picked him up and returned him to the Reservation Halfway House.

He left the Halfway House once again, to be arrested again on a prostitution charge in a big-money tourist area, also close to the Reservation.

My flying buddy asked me to attend a series of Tribal Council meetings regarding the young man. As a result of those meetings, it was agreed that the Tribe would send him to a Native American Rehab Facility---in Alaska. Ever since that day, I have awaited a Subpoena from a certain District Court Judge in Sitka, Alaska. Happily, none has arrived. I confess to mixed feelings over that: I would have loved another trip to Alaska, free of charge. At the same time, I did enjoy being made privy to an unrelated incident occurring on this Reservation:

As is common these days, this particular Reservation boasts a large, moneymaking, casino. On a particular afternoon while I was visiting the Reservation (but not gambling), a Reservation Casino Security Officer, patrolling the casino parking lot, observed a young Anglo lady, richly dressed, sitting in her Mercedes, and smoking the Evil Weed.

As it was related to me, the casino Security Officer approached the lady, who, seemingly oblivious to danger, openly smoked on.

The casino Security Officer calmly stated, "Ma'am, you're under arrest," and began reading the Miranda Warnings to her.

Miss More-Money-Than-Brains laughed loudly and proudly declared that she couldn't be arrested on any

Reservation, since Reservation folks had no authority over non-reservation people. She then elected to provide the Security Officer with a tour of her car, so that he could see for himself that she was, in fact, "In Possession." The tour included the car's trunk, which contained a sizeable quantity of marijuana.

The casino Security Officer thereupon called in the Reservation Police. Miss Clueless continued to dance her you-can't-arrest-me routine.

The Reservation Police Officer handcuffed her, and, while her contraband was being tagged and placed in a duffel bag, she sat, not smiling any longer, in the caged portion of the Reservation Officer's car.

The Reservation Officer took our young lady, sans her now-impounded Mercedes, to the Reservation border. There, they were met by (GASP!) a duly sworn Police Officer from the town located directly across the border.

Don't ya just love it?

## SPIDERMAN

In retrospect, I suppose the young man in academy class 37 that Curly and I came to nickname "Spiderman" was set up by The Fates to perform the way he did. The twenty-one-year-old newly hired Detention Officer had the physical appearance of a military man: medium height, muscular, close-cropped hair, clean-shaven, and impeccably dressed. And he also clearly had an ego that demanded that he must win, at any cost.

Ordinarily, it could have been easy enough to harness the young man's energy and conduct yet another (mostly) event-free Academy. There was present in the makeup of this particular Academy Class, however, a fatal flaw: he was the only male, in the class of twenty new Officers. Worse, seven of the women in this class were very athletically active: three were martial artists, one tri-athlete, one marathon runner, an aerobics instructor, and (I loved it!) a recently discharged Woman Marine.

This sole male member of Academy Class 37 always had an opinion on any subject mentioned during the Academy. For the most part, in the purely academic areas, e.g., Law, Theories of Criminal Behavior, etc., he at least appeared to agree with the Instructors. This gentleman did, at the same time, seem to enjoy contradicting any female classmate's viewpoints. His objections and contradictions were sometimes valid, sometimes humorous, and sometimes totally wacko. The women would often smile, sometimes in a condescending manner, and sometimes laugh outright (which I finally had to put a halt to), whenever he would launch into his typically lengthy and rambling opinions.

The most tolerant, occasionally friendly, woman toward their sole male colleague was the former Marine. She was at this time out of active duty, now a Reserve Sergeant, and was capable of dealing with any issues presented during the Academy, without serious evidence of heartburn. She did locate a seat for herself in the classroom that allowed only the instructors to see her face. During the times I instructed and our lone male student would speak up, she would always give me a "Semper Fi" smile, and roll her eyes.

Our hero appeared to perceive that his shining moments would come during the portion of the Academy dealing with Officer self-defense and non-injurious restraint techniques. He always had something, usually incorrect, to say in any given problem and subsequent resolution presented to the class, whether the problems be grabs from behind, chokeholds, kicks, hair grabs, you name it, he believed he had "The real way" to handle them all. I did direct that he was not to team up with any of the "Magnificent Seven" ladies in our class and for certain not the Marine, nor any of those women trained in the martial arts.

On one particularly fateful day, we had worked for the class long and vigorously, during the morning reviewing self-defense techniques and on inmate restraint and transport. Just before the lunch break, we were dealing with defenses from punching attacks. Let me inform the reader that in a cellblock setting, whenever at all possible, I emphasized the practice of avoidance, or parrying, of an attacker, rather than standing toe-to-toe, and attempting to block every blow coming in. To that end, I recommend a side step and parrying the blow. When demonstrating, I do demonstrate how this particular maneuver will clear a pathway for further restraint techniques as well. Curly and I would demonstrate these techniques with each other, then with class members.

Following our explanation of the problem, the inherent dangers and the possible solutions, our lone male member of Class 37 loudly stated: "I can mess you up before you can stop me!"

The lady Marine smiled at me and winked; being a Marine Corps comrade-in-arms, and having had M.P. and Brig Duty experience while an Active Duty Marine, she had practiced in these very techniques I was now teaching. The other women looked directly at me. Their unspoken question for me was: Well, you old fart, can this guy go right through you, or not?

I admit it; I was hooked. I did advise the young man that if we were going to allow him to engage in this exercise, he should make at least the first few passes at me in a relatively slow motion, so that everyone would have a chance to observe the dynamics of this activity, and also to provide a safe demonstration. He did agree to this; then suddenly he ran toward me, screaming and swinging. I stepped to his right side, parried his blows, and honest-to-god, as gently as I could be given the circumstance, I took him to the floor, where I held him, since it became obvious he wasn't going to stop until he was forced to do so.

The classroom was now silent, except for my male student's labored breathing. I informed everybody at that time we would immediately be commencing on a one-hour lunch break. I released our male student, who I thought at the time had become a True Believer.

After the students were gone, Curly said to me, "My God, Kurt, I thought you were gonna have to hurt him."

I told him, "Man, so did I."

During the afternoon classroom exercises, we demonstrated and practiced one and two-person "non-injurious" restraint techniques, and safe, but positively applied, methods of transporting an agitated inmate to another area in the facility, e.g., to the clinic or a cell. One of the techniques I introduced involved how to deal with a situation where two Officers were escorting an agitated inmate down a hallway to a cell, and for whatever the reason, one Officer lost control of his share of the inmate. The problem I now posed for the class was: how can the Officer remaining at least somewhat in control of the inmate temporarily secure the inmate, so that both the Officer and the inmate will continue to remain to stand, no blows will be thrown, and at the same time the inmate can be physically placed in a position which will allow the second Officer to regain control of his side of the inmate?

The remedial technique is fast and simple if executed by a well-trained Officer. Essentially, the Officer remaining in control will have the inmate's arm and shoulder sufficiently locked so that there should be little difficulty in pinning the inmate, face front, flat against the wall. The second Officer can then step in and regain control of the inmate's other arm and shoulder. With the help of a volunteer from the class, Curly and I demonstrated the technique a few times. Then, with my mindset clearly in "Condition White," I asked the class if anyone else wanted to volunteer to experience the effectiveness of this maneuver.

Guess who volunteered. Yup, you've got it. He sauntered right up to me and said, "I can get out of that, no problem!"

"Okay, my friend," I responded, "How are you gonna get out of it?"

"Well," he said, "When Curly let's go of his side of me and you start to try to place me up against the wall, instead I'm going to run straight up the wall and do a backflip!"

"Say that again?"

"I'm gonna run up the wall and then I'm gonna do a backflip! Come on Kurt, you can't pin anybody who doesn't wanna be pinned. I'm just gonna run up the wall, then do a backflip so I end up behind you, and maybe even put you in a hold. I saw it done in a Bruce Lee movie!"

Lady Marine smiled, rolled her eyes for me again, and walked over to the coffee pot. Curly found some papers on the Instructor's podium that he decided he needed to examine. The rest of the class just stared at me with totally expressionless faces.

Well, here we go: Curly took one side of the young man; I took the other, and we began our trek down the hallway toward the cellblocks. As we had done in prior demonstrations, Curly let go of his side. I was on the right side of my "inmate." With my left arm I countered his attempt to strike me with his left; then, using my body weight against him, and wanting to give him a chance to do his "Bruce Lee" thing, I directed him, slowly but deliberately, toward the wall. At that point, he began his frantic attempts at trying to move his feet onto and up the wall. Of course, he was not connecting at all, and it quickly became obvious that he was not going to. I slowed my movement toward the wall a little more, to give him an extended opportunity to run up the wall. As I slowly moved his body, quietly letting him know he would not able to stop me, he continued to maintain his frantic attempts to gain holds on the wall with his feet, and then with his knees, then---well, "Welcome to the wall."

The young man was clearly tired and very embarrassed. It was time to call for a ten-minute break.

For the duration of the remainder of Academy class 37, the young man, hereinafter to be nicknamed (perhaps a tad cruelly) "Spiderman," rarely spoke a word.

## RAM, THE MIG PILOT

I know this book isn't really about aviation. However, I am a rated pilot, I have been since 1960, and as such, I have an untiring love for good flying stories. I hope that since this is my book, I can be allowed to relate just one very short vignette on a particular pilot who was in one of my Academy classes…

Now, on this subject, allow me to introduce you to Officer Ram, who hails originally from the Middle East. Former Air Force Major Ramallah and his wife were relatively new to the United States at the time they were enrolled in my Academy. He had retired from his former country's Air Force. His wife, a Ph.D., taught a Psychology class at a local Junior College. And now they were employees of the County Juvenile Justice System as well, and attending my Detention Officer's Academy.

While his wife was generally relatively quiet and serious, Ram always had a quick smile. He was quick to offer incisive commentary, often laced with humor. He was not the boisterous "Go-To-Hell" type you might expect from a former fighter pilot and Combat Ace. He was studious, yet congenial, and I would possibly never have known of his background had I not mentioned to someone during a coffee break that I'd love to have flown a MIG-21 (a Russian fighter, commonly flown by all former Soviet countries and their allies from the 1960s to, in a few cases, today.

It so happened that when I'd made that comment, Ram was standing directly behind me. He said, "I have."

I turned to face him and asked, "You have what?"

"I flew a MIG-21, lots of times. It was a good airplane, easy to fly."

Throughout the remainder of that Academy class, Ram and I spent every available minute talking about flying, particularly about the Mig-21.

Ram was one of the more fortunate men from that part of the world. He had accomplished a university education and an air force commission. He had preserved and brought to the United States with him a few physical souvenirs of his air force service; one, a unit patch, now rests in a place of honor among my military paraphernalia. He had graduated from his country's air force flight school, and then served some time in Russia, learning to fly the hottest stuff they had at the time.

His first air combat "Kill" as a fighter pilot had been an American-built aircraft, an F-16. It was hard for me to believe at first, but he did accomplish this feat while flying an older, technically obsolescent, airplane, a MIG-21. That doesn't sound exactly like the movie "Top Gun," does it? It would seem that there would be no way some old, rickety, Russian-built crate like that could beat up on a shiny, new, state-of-the-art American-built fighter plane! Where are the Hollywood scriptwriters and choreographers when you need them?

The answer is very simple: in combat, the airplane will be no better than its pilot. You see, once again, it's all about training!

Essentially, Ram's maneuver to kill F-16's---he did shoot down a few more--- was to enter into a near "Hammerhead" stall when being chased, then he would kick the gigantic MIG-21 rudder to one side, Forcing his plane to heel over; then he'd hose down the passing F-16 with his cannons. Ram's commanders were so impressed with his maneuver and his skill that they decided to remove him from his operational fighter squadron and send him traveling from squadron to squadron, teaching his colleagues this, and other techniques he had developed.

I asked him one day why he left His country of origin. His terse reply: "Politics," let me know that he and his wife had come to a point in their lives where they could no longer abide by the politics of the ruling Government. I probed no further.

# STATE CERTIFICATION

The issue of staff training has forever been particularly tough for the Department Heads of less affluent localities.

When they could, they would recruit people who had an abundance of experience, garnered from other jurisdictions. Otherwise, "training" had to be: Here's your Badge. Here's your key. Go to work." At last, following decades of basically trusting to the Fates in this manner, and only a few years before my retirement, the various Chiefs of Probation and Juvenile Detention from other Counties in my State determined that it would be a good idea to ask the State to budget some training funds for their outfits. After nearly one year of negotiating and collaborating, they, and the State Department responsible for Trial Court budgeting and training issues, agreed on a basic, one-week curriculum to be provided.

The State then was asked to funds and personnel for training and certifying prospective instructors for this one-week training program. At that time, the state decided to require me, my own Academy's Instructors, and volunteers from each of the other Counties to attended a one-week Instructors Certification Workshop, and then to spend another week together to develop training schedules for each County.

Although there were nay-sayers in each department who would not believe that a "one-size-fits-all" training program would fly in an arena where political and economic agendas and rivalries abounded, the programs were generally well-received and the generalized curriculum truly did contain something for everyone.

The one item not included in this training program was crisis prevention; verbal and physical crisis prevention and intervention techniques and physical restraint techniques. This profoundly important element was left out because various County Chiefs had come to an agreement that they would uniformly avail themselves of one of the nationally marketed training programs addressing (or, so the program claimed) those areas.

On several occasions I attempted to discuss this issue with the Chiefs, explaining what I believe are glaring, potentially dangerous, and injurious inadequacies present in that particular program, and in some other, similar, nationally marketed programs as well. I went so far as to provide them all with a manual I had written dealing with these issues, which I had been using for some time to some degree in my own Academy and at other training locations as well.

Although the State's Training Office indicated that they liked my manual, and in fact, they printed quite a few, with my permission, for their use, the County Chiefs said of my program, in essence: "Thanks, but no thanks." In retrospect, I believe the problem was I was trying too forcefully to sell a good idea to people who knew precious little, if anything at all, about the subject of methodologies of preventing or meeting crises in an institutional setting.

Although I did meet with failure on the subject of crisis training, I was confident that we knew Statewide Academy Instructors had a superb new program to present, and we were now ready to put the show on the road!

# HAVE ACADEMY, WILL TRAVEL

Soon after State Certification, we found ourselves invited regularly to take our show, or portions of it, on the road. It often had to be "portions," because each Agency had its time constraints and that demon, Agency Agenda regarding staff training, did creep out from time to time.

We also found that some areas in the State curriculum were best presented by the various counties' local Certified Instructors. This was most often so because each Probation Department, within parameters set by the State Supreme Court, will need presented variations on training themes. It followed in some cases that each Department's Instructors would be in the best position to apply our curriculum to fit their Department's needs.

The various physical Probation and Juvenile Detention facilities, and Detention Division Policies, are different in every jurisdiction. This is particularly true in terms of differences in policy and procedure in the Adult and Juvenile Detention facilities. This being true, Officer and inmate safety and security issues will vary broadly. It has always thrilled me to no end to hear an employee new to the State said: "Well, back where I came from, we did it this way!" Meaning, of course, "Where I come from, we did it right! Here, let me show you, Neanderthals, how to do it." Whenever we had some of these folks in an Academy class, Curly and I would chant together, quietly of course, "Lord, please kill us now and relieve us of this misery!"

So, we, the traveling State Certified Academy Instructors, did our very best to present courses in an appropriately "localized" manner, involving: Criminal and Civil Courts' legal processes, report writing, adolescent behavior, mediation, gangs, resources within a detention facility, interpersonal sensitivity, and rights and responsibilities of Officers and inmates. In our presentations, we were usually very careful regarding what we said, and how we said it, to minimize delivering misinformation or offending any of the local folks, especially Judges and Chiefs.

Sometimes all the Instructors would meet at a central locality and carpool to the training areas. Sometimes we would have to engage in daily round trips (Great mileage checks!), and sometimes we would need to spend overnight at a local motel.

Usually, our classes were presented on-site: in a courtroom, in a jail classroom, in rooms of various sizes, inasmuch as our classes could consist, at any given time, of anywhere between five and fifty new Officers.

My own Department Instructors and I were available as a group only between our own County's Academies.

Although we were scattered all around the State, we tended to be a close-knit team; we communicated with each other regularly, and, although we were commonly several hundred miles apart, we worked on various training projects together. I was twenty-seven years into my career before I had the opportunity to take part in the building of this Statewide Training team, but it was definitely worth the wait.

# THE SUICIDE ROOM

Whether it may be called Maximum Security, Suicide Watch, Special Management, every at least nearly complete jail or prison has a provision for a "Suicide Room." It could be a room specifically designed to prevent suicide from occurring, or just an available space provided to intensively observe an individual who may at the time be prone to suicidal behavior. If there is a medical clinic inside the detention facility, it may well be a separate room within the facility clinic, with a bed specially designed to accommodate mechanical restraints. In some facilities, there may be room for this purpose in each cellblock.

After all these centuries of people searching for and devising a perfect formula for behavior change through incarceration, you'd think, wouldn't you, that if nothing else, we could, by this time of our enlightenment, build the Perfect Jail, right? Well, ol' Karl Marx (no, I'm NOT a Commie) believed that all group decision-making, and, therefore, all group behavior is, in the final analysis, actually based primarily on economic issues. I find it very difficult to find a flaw in this theory. For Government, this translates into: first, "How much can we spend," and then second, "Low Bidder Wins." For private enterprise, this means: "Maximize Profit." Here, I leave it to you to discover wherein the two phrases, "Low Bidder Wins" and "Maximize Profit," the concepts of Officer and Inmate Safety and Security can be found.

I saw these conflicts between safety and economy everywhere I traveled, and at every level within the

Criminal Justice System. I also saw these conflicts in the private Therapeutic Industry's RTC's and the numerous dealings between the two entities. Allow me to provide an example:

Just five years before the printing of this book, one of the Counties in this State caused a new Juvenile Detention facility to be built. It so happened that the successfully bidding architect firm did have a history of designing jails and prisons in other parts of this Country. That being the case, when a Traveling Academy Instructor colleague, who was in the employ of State Juvenile Corrections, and I received an assignment to inspect this new Juvenile Detention Facility, and while there, to provide some training for a few newly-hired Juvenile Detention Officers, I found myself to be looking forward to being exposed to what I was told was the very latest innovations in the field of secure institutional settings.

At the date and time scheduled, we arrived at the main offices of the Probation Department. I was very impressed by the professional qualities of the Chief Probation Officer and the Juvenile Detention Director; especially considering the County they served was mainly rural and not affluent. Both possessed Ph.D.'s and both had substantial backgrounds in the human services field. They were open, friendly, and generous in terms of making every resource we requested available. We toured their new Juvenile Detention Facility, then devoted the next two days to classroom training for their new Officers. Finally, we were given total freedom of the grounds so that we were able to conduct an uninhibited, detailed inspection of the physical characteristics of their new Detention Facility.

When inspecting a new facility for formal acceptance from the builder, one must naturally expect some problems needing to be addressed. There will be light switches with wires not attached, deadbolt receivers not correctly lined up with the deadbolts on doors, carpet not completely tacked down---just expect a mixed bag of, usually, relatively minor details needing to be addressed before the receiving State and/or County Officials sign off on the new Facility and take possession of it.

My Co-Instructor and I had no particular interest in becoming overly excited with these kinds of nitpicky issues, and, although we did expect to find some minor overlooked details, we expected to discover nothing major, since the County had already inspected, approved, and accepted the new Facility.

What we were mainly attempting to do during our inspection was to locate as many areas as possible where inmates could create problems for Detention Officers: places where contraband can be hidden, locks can be jammed, electrical and plumbing areas can be sabotaged, escape attempts could be carried out....

In the end, we located so many places within the facility where it was substantially unsafe for inmates and Officers, both of us were truly regretting the necessity of reporting it all to the Chief and the Detention Director. As could be expected, they did take our report of horrors very happily. Professional as they were, they graciously thanked us for our willingness, to be honest, and direct.

We did discover later on that those Administrators did energetically apply themselves in bringing about appropriate corrections to their new Detention Facility.

Aside from the relatively minor details just mentioned, we discovered three further problems within this new facility which were not just appalling, but, in my opinion, unforgivable for the designers and builders of this facility, all of whom were alleging an extensive history of experience with dealing with detention and corrections facility construction. These were: The Suicide Watch Rooms, the cellblock inmate restrooms, and finally, to make it convenient for inmates to hang their shirts, or themselves, permanently anchored steel hooks attached to a wall in each individual cell.

A Suicide Watch Room was located within each individual cellblock. Each Suicide Watch Room was furnished with a large tempered glass window so that whenever Officers were working in a cellblock they could see inside the Suicide Watch Room without opening the door to the room. Each Suicide Watch Room was also equipped with a surveillance camera. These cameras were to be monitored by Officers working in a central, "Control" room within the Detention Facility.

Each Suicide Watch Room was furnished with a ceramic commode, and a set of steel double bunk beds, anchored to the concrete floor.

That is, a ceramic, breakable with SHARP edges, commode.

That is, a double bunk, I mean, one steel bed located directly over and connected to the lower bed, creating an environment suitable for hanging oneself.

At least there are the surveillance cameras, right? Well, these cameras were permanently anchored within the Suicide Watch Room so that they were immovably focused upon one spot only. It just so happened that the one spot was: the basis of the Suicide Watch Room commodes.

Are you impressed yet? We certainly were.

Now, let's explore the cellblocks' inmate restrooms. They being restrooms, of course, there were no windows built into the restroom walls. This generously affords the inmates privacy from the prying eyes of a Detention Officer while going to the potty. In addition, astonishingly, the cellblock inmate restrooms were furnished with steel doors, also lacking windows.

There was therefore no way for an Officer to be in visual contact and control of an inmate inside the inmate restroom. Yes, I am aware that we are living in an age whereby sensitivity, therefore privacy when desired, is a major issue. How politically incorrect of me to object to this state of affairs.

Better yet, the cellblock inmate restroom doors were also lockable---but only the INSIDE of the restroom door. And, guess what: there was no provision for these restroom door locks to be unlocked by Detention Officers from the outside! In addition, the steel trash container located in the restroom was detachable. Anyone for a little harmless inmate mayhem?

When I returned to my own Probation Department, I looked up my immediate Director and I told him: "Never, never think of having those same architects contracted to build one of our County's new detention facilities." He replied, " Well, I can guarantee that we certainly will not, but you'll be happy to hear that those same architects designed the new State Prison Complex now being built a few miles south of Cordova City!

Once again, this is your tax money at work.

# AWARDS AND REWARDS

The metropolitan area in which I resided and served during my career constitutes one of the largest urban areas in the United States. This means that this area can provide its citizens' quality-of-life benefits, for the most part, of the quantity and quality the majority of the people alive on this planet cannot dream to access. However, there also continue to exist human problems and tragedies with which the rest of the people on this planet are very familiar.

The population of Cordova City and its suburbs is expanding at an explosive rate. A major issue this activity raises is that people who are moving here are often hoping for a new and better life; that the awful problems they have been trying to deal with, unsuccessfully, are being left behind them.

Unhappily, in most cases, such a clean escape just does not occur for people.

Newcomers to Cordova City will most likely bring with them their entire personal emotional, as well as physical, baggage, both good and bad.

At the same time, although the numbers of crimes committed within our metropolitan area have increased, the "Per Capita" rate of criminal activity, that is, the statisticians' "Rate of crimes per thousand people" has not; effectively demonstrating that the "Ten Percent" rule, regarding the good guys-bad guys' ratio, remains intact. The rate of violent crimes against our citizens has uniformly decreased over the past decade.

There, is, of course, no one, simple reason for this. I will say that I do believe a major factor for the decrease in our rates of violent crime, while in much of the Western World the rate of violence is increasing, is to be within the provisions of the U.S. Constitution, and also within the basic character of the ordinary American Citizen. Also, I want to believe that the ongoing relative state of Citizen content in the country (whackos at airports with bombs in their shoes notwithstanding) is at least partly due to your employees working within all phases of the Criminal Justice System.

And, as is true in any other professional endeavor, we who decide on a career in the Criminal Justice System do seek out our own, unique, ways in which to enhance our professional lives. For myself, it was to create and coordinate a Juvenile Detention Officers Academy. In that Academy, I did my level best to promote Officer and inmate safety and security. I was very fortunate indeed to have been provided with this fabulous opportunity.

What I can proudly say about safety and security statistics concerning our Cordova City Juvenile Detention Facilities is that quickly following the opening of the Juvenile Detention Officers Academy, the personnel and Facility involved accident and injury statistics began to decrease. They continued to decrease throughout my tenure as Fearless Leader of the Academy. Additionally, Officer/inmate physical confrontations decreased, and this meant Officer and inmate injuries decreased as well.

The swift and lasting impact our Academy has made in favor of the Department, and therefore the Community did not go unnoticed by the Chief and the Directors within the rest of the Probation Department. At the same time, of infinitely greater value to me was an award I received which had been generated by my fellow Officers: within two years following the establishment of the Academy, I was named, by my fellow Officers, the County's "Detention Officer Of The Year." Then, a few months following this award, the State also elected to identify me as its' "Detention Officer Of The Year."

Yes, I was elated over these honors. Even today, as I stare at them, hanging on a wall next to my military stuff, I feel a great deal of pride. I also wonder: how the hell did I do that?

Throughout my career, whenever people have inquired regarding my employment, their reactions to my response, "I'm a Probation Officer," has never been a simple "Oh." More commonly I get statements such as, "That must be rewarding," or, "I couldn't handle that," or, "I'm glad you guys are doing that work," and an occasional, "Kick some ass for me!" Those comments are often followed by "What do you have to do to be a Probation

Officer?" I will usually describe the education and other qualifications necessary to apply, then I will say: "However, it is true that people who work within the Criminal Justice System, and Law Enforcement, in particular, are born, not made."

I am of the opinion that only a very few personality types will be able to find careers in Police, Probation, or Corrections palatable, let alone physically or emotionally survivable. For those of us who have worked in one or more of these areas, and who have loved the Service from Day One, There could be no other way of life. This is not to say there are no bad days; I did have a few. This is to be expected; but perhaps bad days are to be welcomed, as an indication that something needs to change, and as a challenge to do so.

And, yes, I did have occasions to entertain, even to cherish, an occasional fantasy from time to time, that some Judge, or some Member Of The Bar or some Director was driving off a cliff, resulting in a three thousand foot drop, then into a bottomless pit of quicksand. So, sue me.

*Chapter VIII*

# RETIREMENT

## INTRODUCTION:

As much as I loved being a Probation Officer, I discovered that retirement can be the best part of a career: Now I can write about all those adventures!

## GRASSHOPPER, TIME FOR YOU TO GO!

During the 1970s there was an immensely successful television adventure series named "Kung Fu." Although it was in my opinion a truly exciting series, (after all, my own Styles Marts Styles include Kung Fu and T'ai Chi Chuan), the rather improbable central plot was: "Will an exiled half- Chinese, half-American, Buddhist Priest from the Shao Lin Temple in northern China, having killed the Chinese Emperor's nephew, and being now on the lam from China, be able to locate his American half-brother, who may reside somewhere in the late Nineteenth Century's American Wild West?"

The opening scenes of "Kung Fu" the pilot program depict a very young boy, half Chinese, half American, orphaned, deposited by relatives at the gates of a Buddhist Monastery in Northeast China. The child, "Caine," nicknamed "Grasshopper" by the older Monks, stands before the Abbot of the Monastery. The Abbot extends an open hand, with a pebble in his palm, toward the child. The Abbot says to the child:

"As quickly as you can, take this pebble from my hand."

The child reaches for the pebble, but the Abbot quickly closes his hand and withdraws it. He then says to the child: "When you can take this pebble from my hand, it will be time for you to go."

Within a year of opening the Academy, it became evident that it was going to be a permanent Agency Training Program. The basic curriculum was solid and the scheduling was sufficiently flexible to meet Agency needs. As far as I was concerned, I now had a job that was almost easier than not going to work at all.

The Academy boasted three full-time Instructors: there was Willie, the Probation Officer who had been with me, writing and planning since Day One; there was Curly, the newly-retired cop; and there was me. On a part-time basis, we utilized the services of a number of Detention and Probation Officers who agreed to instruct from time to time. My fill-time partners and I recruited these Instructors; they were not Officers randomly chosen by Administrators, to be assigned to a job they didn't want, or could not perform.

During the time that I was the Academy Fearless Leader, I had to ask only three part-time Instructors to not return for future classes. At no time was that request a reflection on the individual Instructor's competence as an Officer; however, it is true that while some people may have a desire to instruct, not everyone can perform effectively in that capacity.

As to my reason to hang it up, I believe that the problem I encountered which resulted in my decision to retire was very probably set into motion by myself. Many good friends have told me from time to time during my career, that sometimes I can be my own worst enemy, particularly when my delivery in the promotion of a case is more forceful than needs to be. I do acknowledge this observation to be accurate.

As I mentioned earlier in this book, I did write a series of training manuals on a number of issues, concerning Officer Safety and Security. And, of course, I delivered copies of those manuals to the Chief and the Agency's several Division Directors. When it came to the issue of Officer self-defense, It didn't take long for them to uniformly go ballistic.

Do you remember the section in this book entitled "Warriors In Detention?" In that section, I described the initial knee-jerk reactions of many Detention Officers when I began to teach T'ai Chi to a few detained kids: "Good God, he's teaching the inmates to attack the officers!" I think I could safely wager my pension that the Ranking Gods residing high up in Probation Department Olympia did not open the covers of my manuals, much less read any part of them, before they began to shriek, "Good God, he's teaching the Officers to attack the inmates!"

It didn't take long for The Directive to come down from On High: in the area of preventing and handling crises in Detention, I was to teach the approved nationally marketed program that the Statewide Probation Chiefs had decided to approve, and only that.

If by that time they did not know I had no faith in that alleged "training program" whatsoever, it could only be because they had been stone deaf during my numerous presentations wherein I delivered my professional opinions regarding the glaring failings of that program's methods. One Director did tell me that the actual reason for our Chief's decision was that the nationally marketed outfit promises to provide legal representation, should an Officer trained in their program be sued as a consequence of acting in accordance with the nationally marketed outfit's training program. My opinion, which I, of course, did share with the Directors, was that if one if one of our Officers (and of course our Agency, the County, the State) were sued, the nationally marketed company's battalion of attorneys would indeed in all probability appear---but only to maintain as great a distance as possible between the nationally marketed company and the sued Officer, the Department, the State, and so on. The job of defending the County and County Personnel correctly falls on the County's attorneys. Regardless of how hard I apply myself,

I cannot imagine attorneys in the employ of the nationally marked company representing any entity other than the nationally marketed company itself.

Moreover, on the subject of once-in-a-blue-moon training, either by an agency's instructors or by outside sources: Do you recall your years (more for some; less for others) as a junior high school student? Remember those dance classes in the school gym? Remember learning the "Box Step?"

By the end of the school day, could you still do the "Box Step?" Did you care? How about a week later? How about a month later? Six months later? For years I observed my Agency send Officers out to various training programs from outside resources, including this aforementioned nationally marketed crisis training program, allegedly designed to create instructors in the field of dealing with crises. For the most part, those attending the training sessions for instructor certification were there whether they wanted to be or not; whether they had inclinations or abilities toward developing skills in being an instructor or in the subject matter, or not. These newly "Certified" trainers were then expected to train other Officers, whether those Officers wanted this training or not, in a program which, in my opinion, was largely ineffective at any rate.

So, how soon after the training program did the participating Officers forget or disregard the material? More to the point, how soon did the "Certified trainers" forget or disregard the material? Not to worry, says the Administration, there will be an annual, mandatory, refresher class for the Officers, furnished, of course, by the same "Certified" Instructors.

Before the Juvenile Detention Officers Academy, the existing methods of training new officers, exemplified by the scenario I have just described, were pathetic, at best. The Chief and the Directors had been well aware of this deficiency for decades. They at last found the means to budget and create the Academy, and I was the incredibly fortunate soul to be standing in the way when they were searching for a body to heat it. I wanted to change these cynical and ineffective approaches to staff training. Therefore, one of the first rules of the Academy Game I announced was: the training would not be "Academic Pablum;" that is, every bit of information presented in the Academy would be to the point and effective when applied to a work situation. Another rule was that there would be constant, ongoing, sometimes unannounced, training checkups and refreshers for our Officers.

Initially, the Administration agreed to all this. However, Chiefs and other Administrators do tend to be primarily reactive to issues around economics and litigation. And so, because None of those with high rank and power appeared to have the faintest clue or interest in actually workable safe, and effective self-defense and restraint techniques, they chose to believe that the well-hyped national outfits must be entirely correct and I must be entirely wrong. Here, then, was my dilemma: should I disregard my decades of training and the high ethical standards required of professional martial artists, and teach my fellow Officers methods which, in my opinion, were ineffective, and often in themselves dangerous for both Officer and inmate? For most of us poor souls trudging along the pathways of the world of work, the answer to this question may likely be less a response to personal ethical standards and values, and more a response to economic need. And, in fact, most of my colleagues, primarily at the Supervisory level, advised me to just obey orders and go with the flow. However, at the time I was handed this ultimatum, I had a comfortable pension awaiting me, as a consequence of over three decades of service in the field of criminal justice. Moreover, I was also eligible for Social Security benefits. All this meant that at long last I had reached that wonderful point in life wherein I now possessed the economic wherewithal to leave the steel jungle of the Metropolitan City and the concrete heads of the Department Administration, and move to a rural area in this beautiful State while it is still rural.

One evening, I sat on the sofa in the family room of my home, sipping some very excellent scotch, contemplating the decision that I must make very soon. I looked around at my Oriental traditional martial arts weapons and statuary. I imagined myself to be standing before the Abbot of the Monastery at Shao Lin.

The Abbot reached out a hand with a pebble in his palm. I quickly snatched the pebble from his hand.

The Abbot looked me in the eyes, and then said, "Grasshopper, it is time for you to go!"

So, I left.

# FINAL RANTS AND RAVES

So, what happened when I retired? Well, Willie took the reins of the Academy. And yes, the Department did hold the traditional Retirement Wake for me: cake, "Memory Book," plaques, trophies, etcetera. It was nice.

I never had believed that I was irreplaceable, and of course, I wasn't. I never saw a need to go back and visit, so I didn't. I did move to a very rural area. To my surprise, I met several other Martial Artists residing in the area right away, and, at age sixty-six; I continue to teach T'ai Chi and Kung Fu on a part-time basis, in three different local towns; so much for Retirement. In addition, my wife is also a Tai Chi instructor; she teaches classes at a Therapeutic Clinic as well as to Senior Citizens Groups.

And now, please stick around for just a few more pages. There remains some very important information that I have promised to pass on to you. Also, I'd like to try just a little more to convince you that we all need to keep a closer eye on the taxes we invest in the Criminal Justice System.

So, here we go:

# POSITIONAL ASPHYXIA

Say WHAT??? What the hell is "Positional Asphyxia??" Well, I'll wager a bunch that few Criminal Justice Administrators or Officers would be able to define this term for you. And yet, as an Officer or as a staff member working in an institutional setting, you'd better understand what Positional Asphyxia is and how to prevent it, or you'd better vow never to touch any physically acting out person during a crisis!

The term "Positional Asphyxia" describes death as a result of strangulation. Strangulation does not only occur when someone is twisting a garrote around someone else's throat. Death through strangulation occurs when a person is placed in any position so that breathing is no longer possible.

During attempts to bring under control a physically acting out person, the physical encounter can result in the acting out the person being placed into any one of many potentially deadly positions whereby strangulation can occur. Two of the more common deadly positions are the "Choke Hold" and "Hog-tying." Following the death of the victim, Litigation is just one of the other more predictable consequences of this kind of incident.

Positional Asphyxia is not a phenomenon unique to physical encounters with Police, Detention, and Corrections Officers. Death through Positional Asphyxia occurs far too often in other institutional settings, including in hospitals and Residential Treatment Centers. Death through Positional Asphyxia is most often an unintended consequence of an attempt to subdue and control a violent person. All one needs to do to bring about death through Positional Asphyxia is to position a person in such a way to prevent the person from breathing. It's as simple as that.

Positional Asphyxia is easiest to create when everyone involved in a crisis allows emotion rather than training to rule. This is why I wanted the people I was responsible for in the Academy to be able to react according to constant, ongoing training during a crisis. In an institutional setting, reacting appropriately means: being in control of one's mind and body and utilizing a safe and effective method to resolve a presenting problem.

In my opinion, possibly the most incredibly inappropriate reaction to an acting-out prisoner in jail occurred only a few years ago. In a County jail located in a Southwestern State, a prisoner was violently acting out, so that several Detention Officers secured the prisoner into a transport chair. Having been so restrained, the prisoner was then unable to move his body or his hands, arms, or legs. However, the prisoner was able to continue to shout, curse and spit. The Detention Officers' solution was to jam a towel into the prisoner's mouth and then to jam the prisoner's head downward. The result should be no surprise: death by Positional Asphyxia. The resulting multi-million dollar lawsuit has been settled, with the millions of tax dollars of the citizens of that County. Their Sheriff has repeated numerous times that he can find no fault in the behavior of his Officers.

After all, the prisoner was just another hot-tempered druggie.

On a hot summer day in a large city in the U.S. which is plagued by gangs and drugs, a gangbanger who happened to be a diabetic, and a double leg amputee as well, got into a verbal "pissing contest" with a group of

Police Officers. At length, the Officers elected to take the gangbanger down and physically secure him. On the way down, the gangbanger's prosthetic legs left his body. The Police Officers had him positioned face down on the hot asphalt pavement of the street, still violently struggling. At that time, an officer applied a Carotid hold (commonly, but technically incorrectly, referred to by laypeople as a "Choke Hold"). The gangbanger experienced Positional Asphyxia and expired.

Although the resulting litigation was ultimately settled for "only" several million dollars, the original Jury award, following a trial, in this case, was set for twenty-five million tax dollars, to be awarded to the decedent's parents.

Hospital staff has unintentionally caused death through Positional Asphyxia. It has occurred in psychiatric facilities. There have been numerous articles written in professional journals regarding this issue. This problem did not mysteriously crop up only last year. If you can locate no other resource regarding Positional Asphyxia, try the Internet. While surfing the net, look also under "Restraint Asphyxia."

## PRIMARY DEFAULT

"Primary Default" most often explains why and how unintentional horrors such as Positional Asphyxia occur. "Primary Default" means that, during a crisis, a person's mind, and body will react in a manner reflecting the person's current level of training, or lack of training.

The following true story represents what I believe to be as "Worst Case" an example of Primary Default as I can imagine:

Sometime during the late 1980s, following a lengthy Felony Pursuit, four Highway Patrolmen, each driving a solo car, surrounded the subject car, drew down on the two occupants of the subject car, and demanded that they surrender. The two Bad Guys then proceeded to shoot the four Highway Patrolmen dead.

Sadly, there was no lack of indicators of Officer "Primary Default" at the scene of this incident. Here are two:

Empty cartridges were found inside an Officer's pocket; it appears that after firing the cartridges he stored the empties just as would be expected at a Police shooting range, but never during a firefight.

Another officer was shot dead while he was reloading his revolver, one cartridge at a time, just as he would do at a practice range. There were Speed loaders on his utility belt.

Today, many more departments train Officers in more realistic settings, such as "Combat Towns" and the computer-generated "FATS" program. More realistic training such as this is wonderful. It remains, however, that training must be both realistic and CONTINUAL!

Here's a different setting for you: Some intoxicated foulmouthed, screaming, maniac is banging on your very last nerve, insulting you and your companion. You need to be in control of the situation; your companion expects you to "do something," and also the drunken jerk's buddies are daring you to "do something." Your adrenaline is flowing swiftly through every vein and artery. Everyone in the room seems to be moving faster than you want. Now the jerk runs at you swinging both fists! How will you react? The answer is quite simple: you will react in a manner reflecting your most current level of training, or lack thereof. That is "Primary Default."

The big qualifier on this subject is that for the training you receive to be effective, the philosophies and techniques must have been competently presented to you, they must be clear and practical and you must have understood and practiced the techniques, ad tedium, on your own.

Lots of organizations are quite adept at making an audience go "Ooooh" and "Aahhh" with really neat-appearing parlor tricks that they claim to be some sort of self-defense or restraint techniques. These choreographed motions are generally performed relatively slowly and always with cooperative subjects. The next time you have an opportunity to travel somewhere to witness one of these programs, why not ask any professional Martial Artist you may be acquainted with, to accompany you? Then, you can ask the Dog And Pony Show people to work their magic on your friend. Then, you'll have an opportunity to discover the difference between parlor tricks and reality.

A related issue in the area of training has to do with student buy-in to a training program. I can attest that in the fields of Law Enforcement and Corrections if a training program is worthless, the Officers will know it, and in their minds, the program will be eighty-sixed ten minutes after the class begins.

## HONESTLY. THIS IS: THE LAST ONE

Tour any jail and any prison in your locality. Tour your Juvenile facilities. Ride, as a Citizen Observer, with your Police Officers. Examine your local Criminal Justice System's physical facilities. Observe the actions of your Criminal Justice System's Professionals, keeping in mind that none of us have been trained so far to be able to walk on water! Observe the interactions between Officers and suspects or inmates. Of course, your presence will alter these interactions somewhat, but your impressions will likely be accurate. All these experiences will be good for you. Now you will be able to think and talk about your Criminal Justice System with a clearer picture of what "Reality" means to Officers, and why.

Remember, whether a prisoner is a Lifer or a weekender, all but a very few will be out in your communities again one day.

So, how well is your Criminal Justice System, from the Federal Supremes on down, serving you?

www.ingramcontent.com/pod-product-compliance
Lightning Source LLC
LaVergne TN
LVHW011930070526
838202LV00054B/4568